SERGEANT RITCHIE'S CONSCIENCE

Also by Frank Branston
AN UP AND COMING MAN

SERGEANT RITCHIE'S CONSCIENCE

A novel by
Frank Branston

ANDRE DEUTSCH

First published 1978 by
André Deutsch Limited
105 Great Russell Street London WC1

Copyright © 1978 by Frank Branston
All rights reserved

Typeset by
Computacomp UK Ltd.
Fort William
Printed in Great Britain by
Lowe & Brydone Printers Ltd.
Thetford Norfolk

British Library Cataloguing in Publication Data

Branston, Frank
 Sergeant Ritchie's Conscience.
 I. Title
 823'.9'1F   PR6052.R/

ISBN 0 233 96959 4

*For Mother – und den Pohnsdorfern,
ohne deren Geduld und Gastfreundschaft
dieses Buch nicht entstanden wäre*

PART ONE

1

RITCHIE lay back, arms behind head, naked and drowsy in a post-coital contemplation. His inner ear was subconsciously alert to the personal radio broadcasting static on his bedside table. From time to time jocular messages were swapped between the controller and the men on the beat and in patrol cars. As a concession to romance he had turned it off while making love to Eileen, whose strong, bulky body was curled up against his, her blonde head searching out a nerve in his shoulder.

The slight pain was not urgent enough to cause him to move, and anyway his fingertips had found and were caressing a small bump on his shoulder-blade which would, he knew, develop into a boil. It was not right for popping, he decided as he explored its smooth, tense peak, but it would be in a day or two. He wondered how he had escaped such plagues in adolescence only to be afflicted in early middle-age.

He squinted round at Eileen's alarm clock, unwilling to look at his wristwatch in case the movement disturbed her. Two forty-five. He could risk another hour, maybe two, before returning to the police station to see if there was anything which merited his attention. He began to doze ...

The radio crackled, more decisively this time. The controller's voice rang out. It held an urgency which had Ritchie alert and ready to move before a sentence was completed. 'Attention all mobiles. Duty Inspector on talk-through.'

The thin, high voice of Inspector Dale was instantly recognizable. 'All mobile personnel, drop what you are doing and report immediately to me at Kimberley Road. This also applies to foot patrols in the vicinity. Keep an eye out for anybody acting suspiciously but approach with caution. I repeat, approach with caution. Serious incident procedure to be put into operation. Photographer and scenes of crime team to report to Kimberley Road as soon as possible. Who's the duty CID officer?'

A dozen voices on the open network named Sgt Ritchie, who was already out from under Eileen's head and hopping about the floor as he scrambled into his underpants. He ignored Dale's call and threw on the rest of his clothes, which he had piled neatly beside the bed to facilitate just such a quick exit. Eileen stirred but did not waken as Ritchie left the bedroom and ran silently downstairs. He left the house by back door and side gate, giving the cold, dark street that sweeping CID glance that seems so aimless, before sprinting across the road to the parking area of a block of flats where he always left his car when visiting Eileen.

She was divorced, so it was not for her sake that he exercised these precautions, but his. Extramarital sex has been held to contravene the Police Disciplinary Code and, while two thirds of the police force would be in trouble if the rule was rigidly enforced, in which case even single policemen would have to remain virgin until reaching a properly sanctified marriage bed, having a woman on the side had been known to be used against policemen who had fallen foul of higher authority for quite different reasons.

Once in the car, Ritchie called control, giving his whereabouts as an area of town where reception was often bad to cover his failure to acknowledge the earlier signal. He accepted the instruction to report to Inspector Dale at Kimberley Road and drove in at speed, listening to the radio spewing out the instructions which brought the serious crimes procedure into operation. Already Ritchie knew it must be a murder, and an important one to judge by the tension in the voices of Dale and the controller.

Ahead he saw a warning flash of headlights and a white and dayglo red patrol car shot out of a junction, cornering on its doorhandles. Ritchie ignored the red light against him and tucked in behind. Together the cars touched eighty down the broad, straight road.

Expensive shops heralded the town centre. The patrol car swung wide to make a turn, its nose pointing left long before the opening was reached as the driver locked his brakes and went into a controlled slide. Ritchie swore and resigned himself to more sedate cornering. They were soon in meaner streets and after two more corners Ritchie saw the cold brilliance of a forest of blue lights bouncing off the wet walls of the low terraces.

A Panda car was swung across the entrance to Kimberley Road to block it off and a PC was putting up diversion signs. Ritchie pulled up behind the patrol car. 'Mad bastard,' he told the driver and ignored the other's genial V-sign.

Sightseers, pyjamas and nightgowns visible under swaddling coats, moved in to hear the reply as Ritchie asked the Panda driver what it was all about. The driver shrugged. 'Best go and see.'

Ritchie screwed his eyes up against the thin rain and tramped up the road. An ambulance was the only vehicle which had been allowed inside the roadblock. Beyond it was an area marked off with white tapes. Another PC was stationed there to stop all but essential personnel going further. Ritchie hopped the tape. He could see the scenes of crime team inflating a shelter to cover whatever it was lying there. Inspector Dale finished briefing a group of uniformed men for jobs and came over to him. The group parted and Ritchie caught his first sight of the body.

He had been very young, perhaps still a teenager. Blond, good-looking in an immature girlish sort of way. He was on his knees, hands flung forward, head touching the ground like a Muslim at prayer except that his cheek rested on the pavement. His open eyes stared at Ritchie's feet. His helmet had rolled into the gutter and the uniform trousers sticking out from under the quilted raincoat were sodden. The blue light of the ambulance illuminated his face with the last of its strength and made him look drowned.

Ritchie stared at the body sombrely. Life was bloody rough, he thought. He had been looking forward to this week of night duty with its promise of a nightly rendezvous in Eileen's bed. Kiss goodbye to that, thanks to some sprog copper, so new he did not even recognize him, getting himself killed. By God it was hard.

'Found by a passing motorist,' Dale said quietly. 'Can't have been dead long. No sign of a suspect, nor of a knife.'

'Stabbed then?'

'One wound as far as we can see. Left-hand side.'

'Organized a scout-round for the weapon?'

'Only in the immediate area. We've had no time to do anything else.'

Arc lights were connected to a mobile generator and switched on. The scenes of crime team lifted the inflated shelter over the body then swore at the photographer when he made them take it off while he took some general shots to show the body in relation to its surroundings. He allowed them to put it back and disappeared inside for his close-ups. A technician operated a video camera, the force's latest toy, which would allow an instant playback of any moment during these early stages. The police surgeon arrived and earned his fee by certifying that the dead body was a dead body and gave his opinion that it had not been a dead body for long.

'Any word from Pryke?' asked Ritchie.

'Been called. Sounded pissed.'

'If you want him sober, get him before he pours the Scotch on his cornflakes. Can the controller give us a list of messages this boy passed on his shift? What's his name, by the way?'

'Rodney James. Only been in the job four months. Six weeks out of training and still wet behind the ears. Topping's too good for whoever did this.' Dale took himself off, upper lip freshly starched. Ritchie wondered what he thought would be bad enough for the killer. A ritual boiling in oil at Ridley United's football ground? Probably a bigger draw than the football at that.

A dark blue Chrysler Hunter, Pryke's car, eased through the

12

roadblock and drew up just inside. Ritchie got there as Pryke was lurching upright. He staggered slightly, bulky in his overcoat, iron-grey hair looking black and slick in the rain, face booze-flushed. Ritchie shut his car door for him.

'Nasty one, Guv'nor,' he murmured. 'One of ours. A young lad just out of training. Name's Rodney James. Probably a stabbing.' He was not more precise about the injury. Pryke would not be pleased to know somebody had been groping about the body without permission. Ritchie ticked off the steps taken, trying to give the impression they were done on his initiative. Pryke heard him out impassively.

'Spoken to the Chief?' he said, when Ritchie had finished.

'Uniform have done that,' guessed Ritchie.

'Don't you think he might be reassured to know that CID are about when one of his young men has just been killed?'

'Yes Guv,' said Ritchie docilely, knowing if he had called the Chief Pryke would have suspected him of currying favour. Pryke was unpredictable at the best of times, but his temper would be murderous if he had just been woken up after a couple of hours of drink-sodden sleep. Ritchie adapted a joke about a black man's Deep South survival kit — three Yassuh Bosses and a shuffle — to meet the occasion.

He offered Pryke a wafer of chewing gum. Pryke shook his head angrily.

'Might be an idea, Guv, if the brass come down.'

Pryke caught on and favoured him with a small smile as he crammed a couple of wafers into his mouth, dropping the wrappers. They might not kill the smell of whisky which emanated from him in a warm sweet wave, but they would add a touch of mystery. Ritchie picked up the wrappers to prevent them being collected as clues.

People were arriving by the minute. Chief Inspector Hopkins, head of Ridley Divisional CID, Pryke's chief confidant and backslapper, fresh-faced and clear-eyed as though he had just had a good night's sleep and leisurely toilet, was followed by

Detective Inspector Fullalove and Detective Sergeant Gotobed. Hopkins had christened them 'The Loving Couple' and it amused him to have them work together.

Now that Pryke had his retinue Ritchie faded thankfully into the background. He made a mental checklist of jobs that needed doing, of which a temporary incident room was the most urgent. Pryke would need somewhere to operate from while he waited for daylight, when a full inspection of the scene could be made. A house or shop, so long as it had a phone, or better still the pub on the corner. He made his way there, ignoring poly-accented questions, dodging the dogs and their handlers working in and out of alleys. The whole street was on the doorstep, except for the Indians, who watched behind curtained windows.

The landlord of the pub professed himself delighted to be of assistance. Next, a temporary communications centre. Ritchie had a patrol car draw up under the open window of the saloon bar, ready to relay messages on its radio. While he was supervising the position of the vehicle he heard the controller calling him up with the list of messages passed by the dead policeman on his shift. He had died on the second leg, soon after leaving the police canteen following the two o'clock break. There had been no calls since then and only three in the first half.

He had stopped a youth on a motorcycle and radioed in for a licence check via the police computer. The particulars were in order and nothing more had been heard of it. The controller gave Ritchie the youth's name and address and the number of the motorcycle.

Next, a husband and wife disturbance. No action. Ritchie wrote that address down also.

His last call, at one thirteen a.m., had been to a noisy party following complaints from neighbours, just round the corner from where he had died. The address was 38 Mafeking Avenue.

'Spades?' asked Ritchie.

'Good chance round there. Hold on, here's his message. Party quietened down. Neighbour complains that parties at that address are frequent. RC3. Sounds like a shebeen.'

RC (Race Code) one was white, two Asian, three negro. Ritchie looked for Pryke. West Indians were partial to shebeens, bottle parties where an entrance fee was charged. Some also felt undressed without a knife. This could provide an early solution. Ritchie was pleased with himself.

He found Pryke conferring with Arthur Whaley, Chief Constable of South Wessex, whose carefully controlled silver hair shone like a beacon, even from under his uniform cap. Whaley, a temperate man, was struggling to avoid showing his distaste at having Pryke breathe all over him. He touched Pryke's arm and directed him to Ritchie. 'I think somebody wants a word with you,' he murmured and stepped thankfully out of range.

Ritchie ducked his head respectfully at Whaley and waited for him to get out of earshot. Pryke's paranoid belief that people were always striving to place him at a disadvantage made Ritchie reluctant to draw attention to himself. If the Chief had noted that he, Ritchie, had been active, alert and above all sober, while his head of CID was barely able to stand, Pryke would have sought an occasion to destroy him.

'Got something here, Guv'nor,' Ritchie said quietly. 'James was called to a noisy party, probably a shebeen, just round the corner in Mafeking Avenue, shortly before his break. He might have gone back to check on it, walked into a blade and been dumped here. Or maybe he pulled somebody up on his way to or from the party, somebody who didn't want to be searched. Should I take a team and look the place over?'

'Of course you should,' snarled Pryke who was well aware of the impression he must have made on Whaley. 'Here, Hoppy, Ritchie's come up with something. James went to a coon party just before he got done. Get a team together, you, Ritchie, Gotobed, some of these Uniform men – they're standing around like spare pricks – and give the place a good going over. Search them all and nick anybody who gives you lip. This is as likely to be a spade job as anything else. It won't hurt if they get the message that there's trouble on the way until we find the monkey who did it.'

2

'RIGHT,' said Hopkins.

Dale deputed a dozen men, all big hard lads, for the squad. Ritchie sighed. He thought this show of strength was pointless. If James had been stabbed at the party the nearest black would be in Alabama by now. If his murder had nothing to do with the shebeen a show of force could cause a riot. Still, there was nothing he could do about it. If Pryke said to go in mob-handed, that was how it would have to be.

They hit Mafeking Avenue from two different directions at once, half a dozen police cars followed by a couple of vans. The journey lasted only two hundred yards, but Hopkins wanted the team to arrive quickly and together.

The party was showing signs of breaking up. Three West Indian men, their girlfriends snuggling close to them, seeking protection from the iron chill of the night, were chatting casually. Two of the men wore enormous tartan caps. The third had no hat and his hair radiated from his head like rays from a black sun. To Ritchie, in the fraction of time before the group realized they were at the centre of a police raid, there seemed to be no tension in them; they seemed about to follow a night of hard drinking and hard music with a dawn of hard loving.

The arrival of the police cars, tyres screaming under heavy braking, broke up the tableau like a bomb in a shop window. The men started with alarm and one of the women screamed. Afro-hair started to run. Ritchie and Hopkins slammed the tartan-heads against the wall and told the women to stay where they were. They left the pursuit of Afro-hair to the uniformed men.

The black dived down a side alley which, Ritchie knew, led nowhere at all, the uniformed men at his heels. There was a crash of dustbins followed by a high voice protesting. It was cut short by an explosion of breath and a keening moan. The black reappeared bowed over, his arms forced behind his back. He looked sick and there was a drop of saliva on his lips. The coppers held him for Hopkins' inspection. He was a young lad, Ritchie realized, perhaps still at school.

'Nicking you,' Hopkins said, barely glancing at the boy. 'Assaulting a police officer, resisting arrest. That'll do for the time being. See if he's got anything on him.'

Gotobed went through his pockets. 'Why did you run?' he asked conversationally. The boy said nothing. Gotobed poked him sharply in the ribs with a couple of stiffened fingers. 'You gone deaf?'

One of the girls spoke for him. 'He my brother,' she said. 'He afraid our pa gonna whup him if'n he knows he come to this place. Pa don't like parties.'

'Sensible Dad you've got,' said Hopkins. 'Put him in the car. Belt him and save his Dad a job if he gives trouble.'

He lit a thin cigar. Play-acting, thought Ritchie with amusement. The door of number 38 opened a crack and a black face appeared. 'Hit's the Man,' it said. A uniformed body hit the door with a shoulder charge and Gotobed led a navy-blue tide up the stairs. Hopkins strolled upstairs with Ritchie behind him.

They entered a packed, hot dark room. Hopkins switched on the main light and what had been for the past four hours a warm friendly cavern of heavy music, good drink, good shit and fine people was revealed for what it was, a shabby room with peeling leafmould wallpaper, torn threadbare curtains, furniture which had not been good when new, and rotting lino. Coloured paper had been hung round one low-powered bulb to shed a soft, flattering glow on the scene. Reggae thundered at ear-shattering volume through huge amplifiers. Hopkins drew the record arm across the disc and the music ended in a teeth-gritting screech.

The partygoers clapped their hands to their tingling ears and silence fell.

Hopkins took command of the situation quickly, before their bewilderment changed to rage. 'Sorry to interrupt the fun,' he said. 'But a policeman has been murdered round the corner.'

A mass intake of breath was followed by a low murmur. 'Silence please,' Hopkins called, and silence he got, broken only by low thuds as those partygoers to whom knives were an essential item of evening wear dropped them on the floor and kicked them aside. Hopkins was unconcerned. Most of them would have fingerprints and so could be matched up with their owners if necessary.

He told the partygoers to move back. There were sixty people in that room, maybe more. He wanted a clear space between them and his men, or PC James's might not be the only policeman's body on a slab in Ridley Mortuary by the morning.

Some of the blacks did not move fast enough to satisfy Hopkins. 'Get back,' he said in hard tones. 'We aren't fucking about. Anybody who doesn't cooperate has got trouble.'

One man sneered and started for the door. 'One pig less don't bother me none at all,' he said.

Hopkins did not appear to look at him. He slid forward and his elbow swept into the man's ribs. The man bent double with a strangled 'oof'. Hopkins pivoted and swung the man's arm behind his back. 'What did you say?' he snarled between his teeth. 'Say it again, big man.'

The man moaned with pain, his head forced back and his teeth bared, but none of his friends came to his aid. 'Silly bastard should have kept his mouth shut,' was the reaction which communicated itself to Hopkins. Satisfied that he had achieved moral ascendancy over the group, he pushed his victim into the arms of two Uniform. 'Search him,' he said.

He turned back to the party. 'Let's get something straight. We've got a job to do and we're going to do it and I'll nick anybody who gives us trouble. Let's have your hands on your heads. Everybody will be searched, then taken to the police station. You'll be asked a few questions and, if your answers add up, you can go home. Sooner we start, the sooner we finish, so let's get going. Men on the right, women on the left. There'll be some women officers along to search them later.'

A girl called out: 'I'd rather be searched by you than some bull dyke in a uniform, honey. You got such nice blue eyes.' The sally got a laugh, which pleased Hopkins. Laughing people don't riot.

'We're not allowed to have fun on duty,' he observed. His eyes searched the crowd for people who remained tense, noting them for close attention.

The searchers worked fast. Many of the men had cannabis in one or other of its many forms. As each piece was found the searcher would show it to Hopkins. Hopkins let the tension build up for a few seconds each time before shaking his head. 'Another time,' he would say. 'Take his name, though, in case he gives us any bother.'

Each successive release eased the tension and improved the atmosphere. At the same time it impressed the party with the seriousness of the crime Hopkins was investigating that possession of marijuana was not important enough for an arrest.

One of the men Hopkins had marked down came forward, his face tight with anger. He was young and intelligent-looking. His snow-white linen contrasted crisply with his dark-blue suit. 'By what right do you search everybody?' he demanded. 'Where is your search warrant?'

Hopkins looked at him coolly. 'I don't need a warrant. I was invited in by the owner and everybody has agreed to cooperate, you included. It's very nice of you.'

'I have not agreed. You're breaking the law. I refuse to be searched.'

'Hang on, we'll discuss your objections later,' Hopkins said.

'I'm leaving now. If you try to stop me I shall make a complaint to the authorities.'

Hopkins said: 'Hold him, Jack,' and Ritchie took the man from behind, grabbing him by the arms above the elbows and lifting him slightly so that his feet scrabbled at the floor.

'You holding any shit?' asked Hopkins.

He got a fluent stream of abuse in reply. Ritchie jerked the man's arms back. 'Answer the gentleman,' he said.

'No, you bastard,' said the black man between his teeth.

'We'll see,' said Hopkins, and his hand flickered over the kicking man's pocket. 'Search him.'

A PC ran his hands over the man's legs for a concealed weapon, then went through his pockets. He found a three-inch strip of cannabis.

'Thought you said you wasn't holding,' said Hopkins. 'What a deceitful nigger you are. Charge him, Jack. Caution him properly or he'll say we've been careless of his rights.'

Hopkins' amused blue eyes resumed their surveillance of the room. The receding tide had left a flotsam of knives and drugs on the floor. 'Get some evidence bags and pick up those knives,' he told Gotobed. 'Be careful over fingerprints.'

He caught a movement with the corner of his eye and saw a tall thin man feeling in the partly open drawer of a veneered dresser. The man's eyes were on Gotobed, picking the knives from the floor; he did not see Hopkins gliding silently behind him until the detective slammed the drawer shut on his hand and kept it there while the black screamed his anguish.

'What're you hiding, Abraham?' said Hopkins quietly.

'Fuck off, Mr Hopkins. Let me go. I hain't done nuthin'.'

Hopkins jerked the drawer open and Abraham's bruised hand went to his mouth. Inside the drawer were several pieces of cannabis and a flick-knife. Hopkins picked it up between thumb and forefinger and pressed the stud. The slender blade whipped out under Abraham's nose. It was smeared to the hilt with blood, drying but still with a damp red sheen.

A menacing, animal noise came from the throats of the uniformed men and they swayed forward. If there had been fewer witnesses Abraham would not have left the room unmarked. Hopkins dropped the knife into an evidence bag and looked into Abraham's watering eyes.

'Well?' he said.

Abraham whimpered. 'That hain't my blade. I put the shit in the drawer, after I see you charge the other feller, not the blade.' Abraham Lees was a professional ponce and part-time thief. Only a sense of real peril would cause him to make even so small a voluntary confession.

'Is that right, Abraham?' asked Hopkins menacingly. 'Well, isn't that unfortunate? We shall have to dust this for fingerprints and if we find yours we'll know what an untrustworthy ponce you are, won't we?' He turned to Ritchie and a teak-faced constable called Bert. 'Take this along to the nick. No need to be gentle with him. He's not made of glass.'

Bert searched him, finding nothing of interest, and Abraham was roughly frogmarched downstairs and hurled into the back seat of a squad car, yelping as his ear came into resounding contact with the bodywork. The drive to the station was a short one. Ritchie could smell the drying sweat odour of fear. Occasionally Abraham looked about to say something, but Bert's stony profile gave him second thoughts.

They took the lift to the CID floor. Abraham was reluctant to enter the lift and was propelled by Bert's hand planted beneath his shoulder-blades. Ritchie was amused. Must have been nicked by Gotobed sometime, he thought. Gotobed was wont to stop the lift between floors so that he could ask pertinent questions in reasonable privacy. Nothing vicious, a slap or two, and perhaps a hard poke in the solar plexus with a tight-rolled newspaper. Ritchie's hand stayed off the control key. It wasn't his case. Let Pryke do his own dirty work.

Bert had no such inhibitions. A copper had been killed. A few yards away a notorious toe-rag like Abraham Lees was caught trying to lose a knife with fresh blood on it. It might not be enough for a court of law, but it was sufficient reason for using a little muscle, thought Bert viciously. He took the view that the murder of a policeman was reason to spread suffering widely among the criminal milieu and could see no reason why the suffering should not start with Lees. However, with Ritchie there he had to content himself with giving the man filthy looks.

Lees breathed a sigh of relief as the doors opened. Ritchie tripped him on the way out and Bert hauled him roughly along the passage by the collar and dumped him on a hard chair in an interview room. 'I'm leaving you with this officer,' Ritchie told Lees. 'Don't provoke him, will you?'

Alone, Ritchie craved a cigarette. He had stopped smoking years back, but in moments of stress he could still imagine the cool, firm cylinder in his mouth and feel the smoke pulling into his lungs. He looked at his watch. Less than three hours previously he had been in Eileen's bed. It seemed as distant as a childhood memory.

He phoned Pryke, who had already been told of the bloodstained knife. 'No,' Ritchie said. 'Lees said nothing.'

Pryke grunted: 'Set up the incident room at the station,' and put the phone down. Ritchie swore at the dead receiver.

In the reception area Ritchie found the station officer, a sergeant named Clay, coping ill-temperedly, the phone receiver wedged between ear and hunched shoulder so he could speak and type at the same time. He got rid of the caller and looked up, hungry for news. He whistled as Ritchie told him about the bloody knife. 'Might get it cleared up quickly, then?'

Ritchie was doubtful. 'Is Lees the sort of clown who would knife a copper and stick around to see what happens? Don't see it myself, but I may be wrong. What was he like, James? I don't think I ever spoke to him'.

Clay shrugged. 'Bank clerk type. Doubt if he would have stuck it. Bit of a fairy, if you ask me. You know, wet. An educated idiot.'

'Married?'

'No. Don't think he had any girlfriends, either. Wouldn't know what to do with one.'

'Did he ever have any phone calls here?'

'Only from his parents. His Dad called tonight just before he came in for his shift and I told him to call back. James took the call himself: he seemed a bit agitated, as if he was trying to calm the old man down.'

Ritchie stored the information. It was almost certainly meaningless. Hundred-to-one the killer was some petty villain with a knife. There was something about holding a weapon that gave people an urge to use it. But if they failed to make a quick arrest the dead boy's entire life would be the subject of intensive investigation.

Clay said: 'The Yard's being called in, I take it.'

'May not be necessary. Odds are it's a local job which we should be able to handle. Pryke won't want the Yard walking off with all the glory.'

Clay looked at him angrily. 'For Christ's sake, it's not some dosser on the slab. It's one of our blokes. We want somebody put away. Bugger the glory.'

Ritchie yawned. 'We'll get him, so keep your hair on. When was the last unsolved police murder?'

Clay went back to his typing. 'So long as the next one's not in Ridley.'

Men were coming on duty in a steady stream. Not just the six a.m. shift, but men who had heard the news and had come to lend a hand. Policemen are a community within a community. Their work distances them from their neighbours. James may have been unknown to most of them but his death brought in even the idle and disenchanted to offer their assistance. Nothing like a dead policemen to improve morale, thought Ritchie as he borrowed six of them for the incident room.

He requisitioned three rooms: one for Pryke, one for Hopkins and a large one as a general office. Phones were plugged in at the jackpoints and Ritchie filled in a request for private outside lines. He had cupboards brought in to hold statements, exhibits and any property that might be acquired during the inquiry, a vehicle state board with hooks for car keys, filing cabinets, index registers for messages in and out and 'things to be done'. A trestle table was brought in for the 'reader' whose job it would be to comb every statement for significant facts and inconsistencies, internal or external. A mountain of six-ply statement forms was placed on another table, along with a Press cuttings book in which every mention of the case would be filed for cross-checking against any suspect's knowledge of the crime.

He ordered tables, chairs, typewriters, inquiry allocations books, an attendance register, and finally, the holy red pen to be wielded only by Pryke so that anything underlined, annotated or entered in red in any statement or register would be known instantly to have emanated from him. When he had finished he checked what he had done against a Metropolitan Police pamphlet on the organization of a murder room and went to look for Hopkins.

The partygoers were all in the station now, scattered around charge rooms and offices in wilting batches of half a dozen, each with one of the scarce PCs to keep an eye on them. There was a rush for statement forms. Ritchie found Hopkins and told him where he had put Lees. 'Is he our man, do you think?'

Hopkins, his fresh glow waning, shook his head. 'Don't look like it, although the knife was his. It was Porky Rivers's party, you know, quid a head and a bottle. Somebody — Porky doesn't know who, he says — was groping Lees's bird without paying and Lees took exception and took a slice off this feller's arm. Several people have confirmed it so if we can find a spade with a hole in his arm Lees is clear of the murder, though we can put him away for malicious wounding. Let him sweat. If you've nothing better to do, go and tell Pryke the score.'

Dawn was about to break over Kimberley Road when Ritchie got there. He found Pryke in the centre of a cheerful saloon bar roar in the temporary incident room in the pub. Outside uniformed men stamped their feet in the cold and hated CID.

Ritchie delivered his report. Pryke heard about the fight over the girl with interest. 'These coons are lying bastards, all of them,' he commented. 'We'll take it the knife could be the murder weapon until proved otherwise. What about the incident room?'

'All done, Guv'nor,' Ritchie said smugly.

'Fuck me! Efficiency,' said Pryke in wonder, and bought Ritchie a Scotch from a landlord revelling in the roaring, risk-free after-hours trade he was doing.

A pink-faced man with a black bag shouldered his way through the crowd. Pryke shouted a welcome. He did not bother to introduce him. Everybody knew Dr Iain McLean, at least by sight. He had been senior Home Office pathologist for twenty years and had starred in many a murder trial. He too breakfasted on Scotch before Pryke led him to the scene where PC James's body was stiffening under the eyes of Inspector Dale.

Dale made formal identification to McLean, who set about his visual inspection. He pulled out a notebook and jotted down a matchstick drawing of the body's position together with a description. He had a quick but thorough discussion with the photographer about the angles and distances from which the body had been photographed.

McLean lifted the limbs to note the progress of rigor mortis. He asked Ritchie to hold the trunk so he could twist the head to see if the neck pivot had stiffened. 'Rigor commenced but not far advanced. Death between four and six hours ago,' he murmured, motioning Ritchie to let the body down gently. He felt round the waist and jacked down the uniform trousers and flame-coloured underpants. Parting the cheeks of the buttocks he inserted an anal thermometer.

'Couldn't be better positioned,' he said admiringly. He took air and ground temperatures. 'A waste of time, of course,' he apologized, noting the results. 'If he was last seen alive at two thirty and found dead at ... when was it, three o'clock? that fixes time of death far more accurately that I can. You can take him away now.'

The ambulance which had been on the scene when Ritchie arrived finally took the body of PC Rodney James to Ridley Hospital Mortuary.

'I can do the PM now, before rigor sets in fully. You'd probably prefer that,' said McLean, meaning he would prefer that, and a cortege of cars followed the ambulance to the ivy-covered mortuary.

The attendant was already setting out the corpse on the marble slab with the blood gutters. The temperature was near freezing to delay the onset of rigor.

McLean stripped the body and handed the clothes and possessions to an exhibits officer, who placed dry items in labelled bags. Wet clothes were set aside to be allowed to dry naturally.

When James's arm was moved to strip off the vest the fatal wound could be clearly seen, about six inches below the armpit. Finally, when their colleague lay naked, the detectives and uniformed men crowded in for a closer look.

McLean, in rubber apron and rubber gloves, examined the body closely front and back, looking for other wounds. He held up James's right hand to show a deep slash. He peered closely at the wound in the side and parted it. 'A single-edged blade, ye'll notice,' he said in his broad Lowlands accent. 'See the slight vee-shape?'

Ritchie tried to visualize the attack. An upward thrust by a right-handed man, attacking from the front?

McLean inserted a slender probe. He inched it in until about half had disappeared. 'A six-inch blade ye're looking for. D'ye see the bruising round the wound? Clearly the knife was thrust in to the hilt with great force.'

The blade found at the shebeen was barely six inches, more like five, Ritchie thought.

McLean held up the lacerated right hand. It lolled limply back.

'A defence cut. Just the one. So far it looks like an unexpected assault by a right-handed man attacking face to face.' Thus far he confirmed Ritchie's belief. McLean pulled over a uniformed officer. 'Ye're the dead man.' He positioned himself as he thought the murderer must have stood with occasional glances at the body for reference. The video-camera focused on the re-enactment as McLean's hand swept up to his model's ribcage. The PC flinched. 'He wasn't aware he was in danger. He saw the thrust just too late and tried to ward it off with his right hand, probably twisting so that he caught the blow in the side instead of the front. Well now, let's take a look inside.'

With a scalpel McLean slit open the stomach wall with an L-shaped incision and folded back the flap of flesh. The smell of vomit rose to Ritchie's nostrils. McLean put his nose to the incision. 'No odour of alcohol,' he announced. 'A meal of meat and vegetables, and what looks like piecrust – aye, that's what it is, right enough – ingested shortly before death.' He scooped up a mess and showed it round. A voice confirmed that steak and kidney pie had been on the canteen menu.

A young PC, at his first post-mortem, turned white and ran his hand across his forehead. Ritchie's fingers clamped into his shoulder. 'Bear up, son,' he whispered as McLean scooped the stomach contents into a plastic evidence bag and sealed it. Then he laid bare part of the ribcage with his scalpel and proceeded to excise a section of the chest with a saw. The young PC turned away, gagging. Pryke looked up angrily. 'Get him out of here before he throws up over everything,' he said.

McLean gave a tolerant smile. 'Och, he's young yet,' he said over the rasp of the saw. 'I was just the same at the first one I went to, and wasn't that an awful time ago?' He took out the section of ribs and laid back the flesh and membrane until he had uncovered the heart. 'There's the damage, d'ye see?' he asked. Ritchie saw a slit in the wall defined by thickening blood. A few more strokes with the scalpel exposed a limpid pool of blood in the chest cavity.

McLean called for a pipette to draw off some of the blood. 'Ye'll want some, I suppose?' he asked Pryke, who nodded.

The pathologist summed up his findings in technical terms and called for questions.

'How sure are you about the right-handed man attacking from the front?' Pryke demanded.

'Fairly sure. In theory it could have been a left-handed man attacking from behind but it would have been a mite awkward.' McLean demonstrated on his uniformed 'model' again, and it did look awkward. 'If it had been an attack from behind I would have expected the wound to be further back. Besides, how would the dead man have got that defence cut?'

'What about the type of weapon?' asked Ritchie. 'A kitchen knife, flick-knife, or what?'

'I hope I might be able to give you a lead after I've done a section on the wound at the laboratory. Looking at the wound I would say the blade was too thick for a kitchen knife, but don't hold me to that.'

There were no other questions. McLean said: 'Well, that was the interesting bit, now for routine.'

Routine consisted of pulling out tufts of hair from the head, under the arms and the pubic region and taking fingernail scrapings. McLean shaved the head and inspected the shorn skull, chatting inconsequentially the while. 'D'ye remember that case in London a few years back where the dead man, Egyptian I think he was, was thought to have died of natural causes? It wasn't till they shaved his skull they found he'd got five .22 bullets in the back of his head. Amazing that. It was his long hair, fell back into place as he dropped and covered up the entry wounds.'

The mortuary resounded to the harsh grating of the saw biting into James's head as McLean sliced off the top of the skull. He inspected the brain. 'Nice and healthy. Nothing out of place not accountable for by the abrupt cessation of the blood supply,' he said. 'I think that's all, gentlemen. Ye'll have my written report as soon as the laboratory tests are completed.'

He divided up the sample jars containing fragments of PC James's organs, washed and took his share back to London. The detectives went back to Kimberley Road.

It was broad daylight and a minute search of the scene was in full swing. Manhole covers were being pulled up and police frogmen descended, wearing full rubbers to protect themselves from contact with sewage. Strong magnets were being lowered down drains and swished around in the hope that they would produce the murder weapon. Dustbins were being emptied on polythene sheets. 'Found the weapon yet?' Pryke asked Fullalove, who was in charge of the search.

'No Sir. And the dogs aren't helping much. The handlers say it's too wet.'

Pryke's eyes ranged down the street, looking for something to trip Fullalove up on. 'Checked roof gutters yet?'

'No Sir. Not yet.'

'Why not? The houses are so low it would be easy enough to toss a knife into a gutter. You're slow, Fullalove.'

Fullalove bit back the rejoinder that he could only have done that at the expense of not having done something else and went off to do Pryke's bidding.

'Don't think a lot of your deputy, Hoppy,' said Pryke.

Hopkins knew exactly the right line to take when Pryke was in this mood. 'He's not expected to be efficient,' he said. 'He's my Mushroom Man.' He waited for Pryke to cock an eyebrow questioningly. 'I keep him in the dark and feed him on shit.' Pryke exploded with laughter. Fullalove, who had heard, reddened and hesitated, then walked quickly away.

The Press had arrived in the form of Tommy Tompkins, a former local paper reporter, now a freelance. Ritchie knew him well, but they ignored each other. Tompkins approached Pryke, who scowled at him. Their relationship was one of simmering hostility which was always threatening to boil over. Tompkins looked uncomfortable, as a man might when he knew he was going to be publicly rebuffed yet was resigned to going through the motions.

'I understand a police officer has been killed,' he started.

'Do you?' said Pryke.

'Is that right?'

'I've no statement.'

'Well, is it correct that there has been a stabbing?'

'Are you deaf? Or don't you speak English? I said I've no statement.'

'When do you propose to make one?'

'When I want to. And when there are enough Pressmen here to justify my making one.' Pryke knew that this would mean a cut in Tompkins' earnings.

'Then I'll go on the information I've got,' said Tompkins, holding in his anger. 'Are you going to put out a picture?'

Pryke whirled round on him and stared into his eyes with calculated contempt. 'You really are a vulture, aren't you? If and when there is a picture to be given out everybody will get a copy. You're not going to get rich on this case.'

Pryke's look, even more than his words, stung Tompkins to rash retaliation. 'Are you calling in the Yard?' he asked. 'Or handling it yourself, like the Pirie case?'

There was a moment of horrified silence. The Pirie case had not been Pryke's shining hour. He seemed on the verge of losing his self-control and Tompkins recoiled before his angry red face, which seemed to have swollen to twice its normal size.

'Steady, Guv,' murmured Hopkins in Pryke's ear.

He took control of himself. 'Get out of here and don't come back,' he said in an even but deadly tone. 'You're barred from this investigation and if I see you at Press conferences you'll be thrown out.'

Tompkins knew he had gone too far, but his resentment at Pryke's attempts to humiliate him stopped him from trying to make amends. Not that anything short of prostrating himself in the gutter would have mollified Pryke. 'That's like being barred from a vacuum,' he sneered. 'But I'll be there, anyway. I'm the local correspondent for every paper in Fleet Street and if you bar me you're barring them.' He walked away.

'Nobody is to talk to him,' said Pryke to his entourage. 'Nobody. Not a word.'

Stupid bugger, thought Ritchie of Tompkins, why doesn't he learn when to keep his big mouth shut?

Tompkins drove to the hospital and made his way to the mortuary. He rapped on the door and was admitted. In the passage he spoke to the attendant whom he had cultivated for just such an occasion. A five-pound note changed hands and Tompkins returned to his car. He scribbled in a notebook for a few moments, committing to paper all he had just learned, and writing out a story. He drove round to the main block and shut himself in a telephone booth for nearly an hour. By the time he came out he had filed a first-time story which included the name, age and rank of the dead man, the type of wound and the fact that Pryke was handling the case, to the two London evening papers, the Press Association, the local commercial radio and TV, and BBC radio and television. Within minutes, Ridley police station had received the first Press call, and they poured in until they were almost blocking the lines.

Pryke's rage was terrible to behold. There had been a leak. Within minutes of him giving specific instructions somebody had blown the gaffe. Who was responsible?

When no candidate for self-immolation was forthcoming he growled: 'I see I can't trust my own men.'

Detectives scattered to their cars in an uneasy silence which none of them dared break until the car doors cut them off from outside ears. They drove back to the police station, and the search for the murderer of PC Rodney James got under way.

3

An hour later the murder squad assembled for the first time.

There is a confusion, which police and Press do nothing to discourage, concerning murder squads. Most people believe that there is only one, stationed at Scotland Yard. Such a squad does exist but for every murder, other than open-and-shut cases, a new squad is formed, sometimes under an officer from the Yard murder squad, more often not. To a layman, a detective presenting himself at the door as 'from the murder squad' carries the authority of the Yard backed by countless B-movies and sensational newspaper stories. The fact is that the day before he was seconded to the murder squad the detective might have been investigating the theft of a dozen chickens from a High Street supermarket.

The Chief Constable had accepted Pryke's advice not to call in the Yard. With police procedure largely standardized, and the number of twopenny ha'penny forces with insufficient resources to mount a major manhunt cut down by frequent amalgamations, it had become less common to call in the Yard's murder squad unless it was suspected of being a case with ramifications beyond the local boundaries. Cynics at the Yard were apt to say that they were only called in when the job looked hopeless from the beginning, in which case it was handy to have an outsider to shoulder the blame.

Pryke argued to Whaley that all the indications were that the killer was local. What out-of-town villain could be up to something so desperate in an area of run-down terraces like Kimberley Road, where there were no commercial premises which might attract a visiting team? 'Hundred-to-one he came across some tearaway pinching the hubcaps off a car or something,' Pryke said, echoing Ritchie's comment to the station officer. 'We know all the local villains. A Yard man would just be in the way.'

Ritchie had also thought there might be a personal reason at the back of Pryke's mind. It was widely known that Pryke had started his career in the Met before transferring to South Wessex for reasons which nobody had been able to explain satisfactorily. It was certainly not because he thought that police work was better accomplished in the provinces. In his moments of exasperation he had been known to describe his colleagues as 'bloody swedes' and tell them they would not last five minutes in the Met.

Pryke seized every opportunity to visit the Yard to drink with the hard men and discuss new techniques. But he knew he was regarded with condescension, often by men he had worked with in his younger days, for having moved out of the area where it all happened. South Wessex was a nice quiet patch. A dozen burglaries a week constituted a crime wave and such violence as took place was normally domestic in origin or the consequence of Saturday night revelry. True there had been that mad bastard a few years back, the case Tompkins had referred to, who had killed three people over a land deal, but the less said about that the better. Apart from that it must have been ten years since they had a murder of any consequence, and Pryke, whose sense of humour was at its most deficient when it came to jokes against himself, found it galling to be asked why he was interested in new methods. 'All your boys need is a magnifying glass and a bullseye lantern, ain't it, Cyril?'

But a murdered policeman rated headlines. And Pryke did not want his Yard drinking partners to claim he came running to them as soon as he had a decent case.

The big room Ritchie had requisitioned was packed and the air was thick with smoke. Divisional chiefs had been generous with their men for this job, and eighty detectives were crammed into the room, greeting old friends and swapping good-natured insults. A few uniformed men were present, one of whom was Inspector David Nicholas, by common consent the dirtiest policeman and best reader in the business. Nicholas was a uniformed inspector in the statistics department which consisted of himself and a girl. He was grey-faced with tobacco-stained brown teeth. His lank hair showered his shoulders with dandruff. Despite Pryke's contempt for Uniform Branch, a murder squad without Nicholas was unthinkable. In one case he had read sixteen hundred statements before picking out two which conflicted. One of them had been made by the murderer.

Dale was up front, nose in the air, observing the detectives with much the same disdain as he would reserve for a coachload of drunken football fans. With him were two young PCs, friends of the dead boy's, Ritchie assumed, awestruck at being pitched into this drama so early in their careers. A group of detectives from other divisions was clustered around a six inch to the mile map of the district around Kimberley Road to familiarize themselves with the area. Ritchie looked at it too, although he knew it well enough. It was old and working-class, with a multi-national population. Door-to-door inquiries would be a bugger, he thought, but at least the railway line, which acted as a stopper at one end of the street, would provide a limit to the door-knocking inquiries in that direction.

Pryke entered behind Whaley and the room fell silent. Whaley waved down the men rising to their feet, and acknowledged Dale, who had come smartly to attention. Tall, with shining silver hair and ruddy, blunt features, Whaley looked more like a hunting squire than what he was, one of the top police theoreticians. He was distrusted by many of the men, who had marked him down as a 'political' copper, more interested in the theory of policework and altering legislation than in the nitty gritty of enforcing the law and maintaining order.

Whaley spoke first: 'I do not need to tell you that the murder of a policeman is something we are not prepared to tolerate. That applies to any killing, indeed any offence, but to us the murder of one of our own kind in the course of his duties has special relevance and importance. The fact that the victim was a young lad, at the beginning of his career and unknown to many of you, does not diminish this. Rather it makes it more poignant.

'At the same time the fact that he was a policeman lays a special responsibility on us. The country will be watching to see how this case is handled. Those who always seek to criticize the police will look for signs that we have allowed our feelings to get the better of us. If there is a scuffle in an arrest and a suspect is injured they will be ready to allege brutality. If there are any irregularities in interrogation or identification there will be allegations that we have tried to "improve" a weak case.

'Therefore, gentlemen, let there be no short cuts in this investigation at any stage. Allow the fact that the victim was a policeman to affect your energies, but not your judgement. Then, when the man responsible is found, as I have no doubt he will be found, we may face the world with a clear conscience. Should anybody then try to point a finger at any of you, you will have my full support. Thank you, gentlemen. I would say "Good luck", except that I hope luck will not have any part to play in this case.'

Whaley nodded briskly to Pryke, who came to a semblance of attention, and left quickly, leaving the squad with the clear understanding that if they did not play it by the rulebook they would not get any support from him.

Pryke's face was thunderous. He drew a deep breath and said: 'Well, you heard. Now let's get on with it.'

Pryke summarized the progress of the case from the first message received. 'The deceased was Rodney Christopher James, aged nineteen, a police constable stationed at Ridley. He was unmarried and lived with his parents at 121 Wyngard Way, Ridley. In the job sixteen weeks almost to the day, commenced beat duties six weeks ago after completing ten weeks training. We'll hear from Inspector Dale, who was his section officer, and some of his colleagues later.

'His body was found on the pavement outside 73 Kimberley Road, which is here ... ' Pryke pointed to the six inch to the mile map. 'This was part of his beat. It was discovered by a motorist, Mr Sydney Lewis of 46 Ladysmith Road, who was on his way to his home just round the corner. Time of first message was 0257. Lewis was a bit reluctant to say what he was doing out at that time of the morning, but eventually admitted that he had been with a woman friend living at Keynsham. We are checking that, of course, but there was no sign of blood on him and no apparent reason for him to stab a police officer, so we think he is probably in the clear.

'According to Inspector Dale, James should have reached that point on his beat very soon after resuming his patrol following his break, which leaves us with several possibilities. He could have been dead for twenty minutes or so before he was seen, or he might have been held up earlier on his beat and thus been late in arriving at that point, or he might have been alerted to some suspicious circumstances and stayed to keep observation or deal with the matter. If the latter, it probably did not seem to be particularly significant or he would, presumably, have radioed in for assistance.'

Pryke went on to describe McLean's findings at the post-mortem and the negative outcome of a search of the area. Interviewing residents would take priority, the task to be coordinated from a mobile incident room which would be towed to Kimberley Road. 'The street is populated mainly by coloureds of all descriptions, together with some Europeans of Irish and Continental extraction. There are very few English and we may experience a reluctance to cooperate. If so, impress the gravity of the matter on the persons concerned very forcibly ... but entirely within the limits set out by the Chief Constable, of course.'

Pryke was rewarded by a low laugh and permitted himself a brief smile before dealing with the next point. 'Some of you will know we raided a shebeen nearby in the early hours. This has produced a confirmed case of malicious wounding. A knife with bloodstains on the blade was found. Fingerprints show it was handled by Abraham Lees, whom many of you will know as a small-time West Indian pimp. The blood has not yet been typed so we are keeping an open mind, but witnesses say there was a fight at the party in which someone was stabbed. If this is so presumably Lees will be out of this case, although we'll no doubt charge him with the wounding. But don't forget the party. There is a strong possibility that the killer was one of the men or even a woman at the party. It could have been somebody on his way home whom James stopped to search. If he was carrying a knife, or drugs, or was just stoned out of his mind, he might have killed James to avoid prosecution. So be very thorough in questioning any West Indians, check with their families if they were at the shebeen, whether they went out and at what time they returned.'

After commenting on the possibility that James had come across a burglar or somebody breaking into a car, Pryke added: 'James's parents have been informed by Mr Whaley of the death of their son. They have not been formally interviewed yet but state that their son had no personal enemies or emotional entanglements to the best of their knowledge. They state that he was well liked by everybody. We will now hear from Inspector Dale.'

Dale – blond, humourless, young for his rank and marked out for the top – started with unaccustomed hesitation. 'I suppose the most significant thing about James was his insignificance. I don't mean he was unintelligent, certainly not that. He attended Thomas Hardy Upper School and came away with six O-levels and one A-level. Academically he was top of his intake and with two more A-levels would probably have gone to university instead of joining the police. He was a good sportsman with an emphasis on athletics rather than contact sports like boxing or rugby. His training marks were good except that he scored low on leadership qualities. If he had lived I would have expected him to become a specialist of some kind rather than achieve command rank, although he might have developed leadership qualities in due course.'

Ritchie commented sourly to himself that, on the contrary, James seemed to have all the qualities required for the highest ranks in the modern police force — facelessness combined with academic ability.

Dale continued: 'His colleagues say he did not discuss girlfriends or join in bawdy talk. He attended church but was not a Bible thumper and seemed most animated when discussing schooldays or talking shop. Having decided on a police career he threw himself into it wholeheartedly. Experienced officers found him naive to the point of simplicity and he was the butt of a few mild practical jokes which he took in good part. I don't think there is a lot more I can tell you, but I have here two lads who joined the force along with him who might be able to tell you more.'

The two teenaged PCs, overawed by the mass of leathery CID faces, were suffering from stage-fright. In the end one said: 'The Inspector's got it about right. I would say Rodney was very shy, like. I think he wanted to make friends but didn't know how to go about it. But everybody liked him. You couldn't not like him, you know? He was always ready to help anybody who found the classroom stuff difficult. He was shit-hot on that.'

Fatally, the other young PC felt compelled to make a contribution: 'We called him "the Virgin" because he seemed embarrassed when we'd talk about women. And he was sort of prudish in the showers ... ' There was a titter and the young PC, in his confusion made things worse: 'I mean ... I don't mean there was anything wrong with him, just, er ... ' He caught Dale's angry stare and trailed into blushing silence.

Pryke enjoyed the boy's discomfort. 'Now we know what his, er, friends thought of him. No truth in the rumour you're transferring into the Diplomatic Corps, is there, son? Pity. They need blokes like you. Well, that's PC James, or was. Quiet, intelligent, unassertive, good-natured, religious and a bit poofy. More'n likely it's got nothing to do with the case. Any questions for Inspector Dale or these lads before they go? No? Right, let's have the collater.'

The collater, the officer in charge of criminal intelligence in Ridley, told the squad: 'PC James had not been in the job long enough to show particular strengths and weaknesses, but he seemed observant enough, particularly where the "target" criminal programme was concerned.'

The target criminal programme was a sensitive subject. Every week or fortnight a 'target' was chosen, a criminal with a long record or somebody suspected of being involved in crime. The target would not normally be under investigation for any specific offence, just somebody of interest. His name, picture and description would be circulated, with instructions to watch out for him and report whereabouts, associates, vehicles, changes of address, girlfriends and other information. The object was partly to imprint the names and faces of known criminals on the memories of policemen, partly to provide up-to-date criminal intelligence and, once in a while perhaps, catch a target in an unlawful act.

Civil liberties groups were opposed to the 'target' programme on the grounds that it meant spying on people who were not known to have committed any crime and that there was an inherent risk of guilt by association for anybody, however innocent, who might be seen in the company of a target. Nevertheless, the system was considered too useful to be dropped.

The collater said: 'We've had four targets since James joined us. The first was Noel Ralph Johnson, born 8-12-51, convictions for theft, possession of dangerous drugs, assault on police, resisting arrest, possession of an offensive weapon – and, yes, it was a knife – and GBH. Obviously of interest in this case although the assault on police was not a particularly serious one. He kicked an arresting officer in the shins and tried to escape.'

Johnson, thought Ritchie, who had once arrested him. By God, I'd like it to be him.

'The next one will be of particular interest. Abraham Lees, born 9-4-39 in St Kitts, came to this country in 1956, two convictions for living on immoral earnings, one for malicious wounding, the result of an attack on one of his women who was trying to break away from him.

'The third, current until Saturday, was Archibald Loach, born 3-2-48, two convictions for larceny as a juvenile, nothing since then but known to be a conman and organizer of unlawful gaming parties. No reputation for violence.

'The current target is Hector Harold Tomlinson, born 27-9-34, convictions for store- and safebreaking, a fairly high-class thief, no convictions for violence or reputation that way. Lives in Totley, the opposite side of town from the murder scene, and in my view wouldn't be seen dead doing a job in Kimberley Road ... '

Pryke growled: 'If you were a detective you'd be in CID. Leave the conclusions to us, Sergeant.'

'Yes Sir. Well, that's the four. James reported two sightings on Johnson, one on Loach, none on the others. The only other report he put in to me was on a man he believed to have been disqualified from driving he had seen at the wheel of a car. Turned out the man was appealing against conviction and his licence had been returned to him pending the hearing.'

'Had he made any arrests?' asked Hopkins.

'Two motoring offences. Purely minor, but I've got the details here if you want them.'

'We'll check them out,' Pryke said.

An out-of-town detective asked: 'What about these targets? Is it a bit odd that he should sight Johnson twice when he had got only one sighting on the others combined?'

'Not really. James's beat took him through the town centre past the Arcade Cafe where the hard drug users hang out.' The collater shuffled his papers. 'Here we are. Yes, one of the sightings was at the Arcade and the other was when James was off-duty. He saw Johnson with his girlfriend, Alison Parker, at Ridley station. Nothing particularly odd about that. He spotted Loach leaving the Royal George with a crowd. The Royal George is where the big spenders hang out.'

There were no other questions and the collater left.

'Right,' said Pryke. 'Ideas and suggestions.'

Ideally a murder squad functions democratically. The Guv'nor controls the investigation, of course, but with everybody from the greenest Temporary Detective Constable to the hoariest old 'seen-it-all' detective feeling free to put his penn'orth into the pot. But Pryke's baiting of the young PC made many of the detectives reluctant to speak in case they became the butt for ridicule.

Slowly the ideas started coming in, most of them the names of criminals the contributor felt ought to be hauled in for questioning. Pryke said a list was being prepared by the collater. Suggestions should be passed on to him.

Hopkins called for an urgent check on the ownership of all vehicles parked in Kimberley Road at the time of the murder. From the time the body had been discovered no vehicle had been allowed out without its number and the identity of its occupants being established.

Another voice called for a check on all vehicles entering the street until further notice. 'The killer might have had regular business in the street.'

Ritchie asked for a check via the Home Office for the names of all Ridley-based criminals recently released from jail. 'Might have been somebody who's just done a long stretch and knew that if caught again, even on a petty job, he would fall for several years.'

'Somebody on a suspended sentence?' put in Fullalove.

'We'll check,' said Pryke.

'What about somebody trying car doorhandles, trying to nick a car for a job or a joyride, or just to get home in? The Shepherds

42

Bush job, you know, when those three coppers got shot, that was some team looking for a getaway car for some piddling little job,' offered a young detective. 'Suppose we took prints off the doorhandles?'

'Why don't we shut our eyes and stick a pin in a list of names?' said Pryke. 'If there are no more sensible suggestions let's get going. Uniform will help in door-to-door inquiries. Somebody had better go and see James's parents and handle background inquiries. Ritchie can do that, but don't take too long over it. We'll have an all-CID team picking up possible suspects. And in addition I want the word to go out that life is going to be very hard, very cruel, very nasty for every villain in Ridley until this job is cleared up, so that it will be in their own interests to help us put this bastard behind bars.'

Hopkins closed the conference by outlining administrative arrangements and allocating men to specific tasks. 'Get some sleep after you've seen the parents,' he told Ritchie. 'I want you to do a tour of your snouts tonight.'

Ritchie read up James's personal file. Father a buyer for a chain store, mother a housewife, did some voluntary work at Ridley Hospital. No other children. The thought of interviewing the parents held no terrors for him. He had done it too many times. Better this than delivering 'messages sympathetic', telling the next-of-kin of the death or injury of their loved ones, generally by accident or violence. Sometimes the smell of boiled cabbage recalled to his mind the awful night when he had delivered his first, telling a mother that her two children had drowned on a canoeing holiday in Wales. God, how that woman had shrieked and shrieked and held her head as though it was bursting as the vegetables boiled over in the kitchen behind her and her husband came running down the stairs with a towel round his waist thinking she was being murdered. Ritchie had staggered back to the polce station, weeping, and almost resigned there and then. Even now, after two decades in the police force in which he had seen almost as many varieties of horror and grief as existed in

43

the world, the memory of that first message sympathetic was something to push out of reach at the back of his mind.

James had lived in a semi-detached private house, built shortly before the war. Ritchie's knowledgeable eye concluded that the family had lived there for many years. When young couples move into an old house they usually modernize everything, after which it stays the same until death or removal brings about another change of tenure. This house had not been touched for twenty years, apart from repainting. The bell-push, an old-fashioned white tit in brown plastic, didn't work. A young PC, stationed at the house to ward off the Press, opened up to Ritchie's knock.

'How're they taking it?' Ritchie asked in a low murmur.

'He's not so bad. She went to pieces and is under sedation.'

A big man in grey late middle age looked out from one of the doors opening on to the hall. He looked broken. Ritchie introduced himself and a damp flabby handshake was exchanged. Mr James led him to the room from which he had emerged. It was small, crowded with furniture. On one wall were pictures of urchins with enormous eyes. The other three walls were papered with a representation of hand-hewn stone faced with wrought iron in a three-dimensional effect. As Ritchie looked at it the pattern seemed to move. Not a room to get drunk in. On the mantelpiece was a framed photograph of Rodney James in civilian clothes. It would stay there over the years, the clothes growing more clearly old-fashioned until a visitor would know at a glance that the young man in the picture was dead.

James asked if it was necessary to call his wife. She had recovered from the initial shock, he said, but he did not think she was in any condition to be interviewed. Ritchie told him she would have to be interviewed eventually but he could call back. James nodded. 'It might be better.'

Ritchie had discovered long ago that when interviewing grief-stricken people it was more painful to beat about the bush than confront issues head-on, so after hearing what a fine son Rodney had been, how he had never given them any cause for anxiety and how determined he had been to be a good policeman, Ritchie started probing into the boy's background, including his sex life.

Had he any girlfriends?

James hesitated slightly before answering: 'Not really. He was a little too young for that sort of thing.'

Ritchie, whose initiation had taken place on Totley Common when he was fourteen, with a girl who was a year younger but whose experience was ageless, cocked an eyebrow. 'None at all? Girls and boys get together far younger than they did in our day, you know.'

James shifted uncomfortably. 'Well, there is Marilyn over the road. He used to take her to church dances. And at school, when they had a disco, she used to go with him. But I don't know that she was what you would call a girlfriend. More a friend who happened to be a girl.'

Ritchie looked at him meditatively. Was he worried that his son might be queer, he wondered. And should he ask? Had the murdered man not been a policeman he might have done so, but would James complain to the Chief? Time enough if it proved relevant.

Had James noticed anything strange about his son's behaviour lately? No. Any reluctance to account for his movements? No, James said again. They had always known where he was, whether on duty, or in a training session, or going to the cinema with Desmond Hagley, Rodney's old school friend. Ritchie took his name and address.

He pressed on with his questioning until he reached the conclusion that PC Rodney James had been a remarkably boring person. So boring he scarcely believed it. It was only when he asked whether the dead boy had ever discussed his work that James said something interesting.

'He told us he was keeping an eye on somebody called Johnson, a drug pusher. His parents lived round here once, a long time ago, and we knew them vaguely. Rodney had known him at school, although Johnson was about three years ahead. Apparently he was a terrible thief and bully. Rodney seemed to be quite pleased to be keeping an eye on him.'

It was the first potentially useful piece of information the interview had elicited. Ritchie got some statement forms out of his briefcase and took down James's words in the stilted form which passes for colloquial English in the police force. It took a long time. James had last seen his son alive at nine thirty on the eve of his death when he left for his ten o'clock shift. Ritchie reminded him that he had phoned Rodney at the station. What was that for? It was to tell him to bring home some cigarettes.

The door opened and Ritchie heard a hesitant footstep. He turned and saw a small bewildered woman, clasping her hands in front of her withered bosom. Her frizzy pepper and salt hair was unkempt. 'My wife,' said James, and introduced Ritchie.

She was in no state to be interviewed. Ritchie wrapped everything up as quickly as possible, took a note of the name of James's last form master at school and escaped, and promised to be in touch the moment there was any news.

4

EXHAUSTION was beginning to show in Ritchie's face by the time he got home, his eyes feeling like iron balls, his stomach rumbling with hunger, not knowing which he needed first, food or sleep.

After leaving James's parents he had looked in on Marilyn, a mousy little thing with too much chin and nose. He wasn't surprised to learn that she was a regular churchgoer and Sunday School teacher. You could always tell them, he thought. She had little to add to the picture of Rodney James as a colourless youth who took life and himself too seriously. They had teamed up for school dances and church socials, but there had been nothing more to it.

'It was our parents, really,' said Marilyn, as though she had to find an excuse for being seen out with a boy. 'They were friendly, so we were sort of thrown together. But that was all we had in common.'

She had never seen him out with another girl, nor with anybody, for that matter, except his parents, or Desmond Hagley, or a school group.

Ritchie went back to the murder room, filed his reports and statements and booked out for a rest before he started again that evening. Janet, her feet in woolly carpet slippers, her hair trailing down her face in rat-tails, was surprised to see him. Surprised, but not pleased. But that was normal.

'I thought you'd be on the murder squad,' she greeted him. 'I wasn't expecting you for hours.' Ritchie explained briefly that he was expected to go out on a round of his informants that night, that he planned to get some sleep and perhaps she could refrain from using the vacuum cleaner within earshot while he was doing so.

Janet sniffed and eyed Ritchie meanly. Daughter of a chief inspector, with two brothers in the force, both younger but higher in rank than Ritchie, she was aware that promotion in the police force meant passing exams and going by the book; without that, having the best informants in the force meant nothing. Ritchie was a 'good thief-taker', the CID's highest accolade. But to Janet's father the CID were 'those cowboys'.

Ritchie observed the expression on her face and drew the correct conclusion. 'You should have married Dave Nicholas,' he said, knowing her aversion to the insanitary statistician. 'A wonder between the sheets, so they say. So long as they come in a loose-leaf binder. And what about some food?'

She started cooking with the same lack of enthusiasm she applied to most things. 'Tompkins rang,' she said, between dealing with pans, eggs, sausages and fried bread. 'He wants you to call him back. I don't know why you talk to him, honest I don't. Pryke'll slaughter you if he finds out.'

'If Tompkins keeps his mouth shut, and you keep yours shut and I do the same, Pryke won't find out, will he? Tompkins is sometimes useful to me and I'm sometimes useful to him.' But not this time, he thought, dialling Tompkins' number and remembering that morning's scene.

Tompkins answered almost immediately. They exchanged ritual insults before he asked: 'What's the score?'

'Well, you're as popular as a leper with the clap, if that's of any interest. Did you break the story?'

'Who else?'

'Where'd you get it from?'

'Don't be daft.'

'You're probably screwing fat Florrie in the canteen. She knows everything that happens. But Pryke thinks it's one of us, and if he finds out who he'll have his balls for breakfast.'

'Pryke can stuff himself. What about a meet? I could be

persuaded to buy a pint.'

'Sorry. This one's too close to home.'

'Pity. I won't be able to tell you about the complaint against you.'

'Complaint' is an unpleasant, marrow-freezing word in the policeman's lexicon. 'What complaint?' asked Ritchie.

'I'll be in the Rose in half an hour.' Tompkins put the phone down and Ritchie swore into the receiver.

After wolfing his meal, and ignoring Janet's comment that she thought he was going to bed, Ritchie arrived at the Rose. Tompkins was the only other customer. Without asking, he bought Ritchie a pint and they found a corner.

'Well, what's this about a complaint?'

Tompkins took a pull at his beer. 'Were you in the spade party raid?'

'What raid?'

'If you weren't you've got a double who grabbed a small, balding guy who got nicked for possession. Well, that little runt is a member of some race relations outfit who was visiting his brother who took him to the party ... ' he had all of Ritchie's attention now '... and he has reported it to his organization, who are planning a showpiece complaint to demonstrate how the bigoted police deal with blacks. The complaint also includes some youngster who claims to have been duffed up outside and another fellow Hopkins is supposed to have assaulted.'

'How do you know?'

'Can't reveal sources,' said Tompkins. In fact he had been put on to it by the news desk of *The Guardian*, to whom the race relations outfit had leaked it, but Tompkins knew that if he revealed harmless sources it would allow conclusions to be drawn about sources which were more sensitive.

'Take it from me,' he said. 'It's straight up.'

'How do I come into it?'

'This bald geezer whose name – would you believe? – is Black, claims his arms were pinned behind him by some big ugly bastard in plain clothes, with a broken nose, short, straight hair, and close-set, piggy eyes. Flattering, I would say, but recognizable. He says that while this thug was manhandling him, somebody else who sounds like Hoppy planted some shit on him. Would that be about right?'

'He's daydreaming. He tried to duck out without a search so I stopped him. He wasn't planted. Are you doing a story? Do me a favour, then. Leave me out.'

Tompkins had no intention of jeopardizing a useful source, but he tried to use the request for leverage.

'I'll see what I can do. What about the murder itself? What's the thinking about it?'

Ritchie had no intention of paying Tompkins' price, being sure the other wouldn't mention his name.

'Early days,' he said. 'We're slogging through routine. If Pryke's got any cards he's playing them close. I'll give you a shout if anything breaks.'

He finished his beer, left a dissatisfied Tompkins and returned to the squad room. Dave Nicholas was alone, wading through the opening avalanche of statements.

'Rubbish,' he said, indicating the ones he had dealt with. 'Not worth a light.'

'Anything come out of the shebeen raid?'

'Only that it's blown up in Hoppy's face.' He looked sharply at Ritchie. 'You don't seem surprised?'

'I heard some monkey might be making a complaint.'

'A complaint? More like a terminal illness. Not from some ignorant nignog off the dole queue, either. This one's from some college-educated snooper with the Race Relations Board or something. He's getting at us both ways. Not just for planting and assault, but for not charging people who were actually carrying drugs and weapons. The Chief has got Pryke and Hopkins in with him now. He must be doing his nut after his performance this morning.'

Ritchie took some comfort from the fact that Nicholas had not

50

mentioned his part in the raid. Probably Tompkins had been trying to get him going in an attempt to lever some information out of him.

He drew Nicholas's attention to the line about Johnson in the statement made by the dead policeman's father.

Nicholas whistled. 'Tie that up with what the collater said and Johnson begins to look very, very interesting.'

Nicholas's estimation of Whaley's reaction to the raid was mistaken. He did not like it, of course. No Chief Constable likes to get involved in the wasp nest of race relations. Yet, in a less charged case, he might have welcomed the incident. Now, as he faced Pryke and Hopkins over the broad maroon of his Morocco surfaced desk, his concern was over how far he dared go in exploiting the CID's bull-headed tactics for his own purposes.

Whaley did not like Pryke. More important, he did not like the kind of policeman Pryke represented. Pryke, in his view, personified all that was bad about the CID.

Whaley had spent most of his service in the Uniform Branch of the Metropolitan Police, refusing to transfer to CID because of the deep suspicions he harboured of the detective barons of the Met. He had climbed through the Uniform Branch, listening to the reports and rumours which filtered out of the state within a state which constituted the Met's Criminal Investigation Department.

In his view, crime writers, fictional or otherwise – he thought the distinction largely spurious – had contributed powerfully to building up a false image of the CID, propagating the myth that all policemen loathed a bent cop at the same time as the Fleet Street crime reporters contributed to corruption by buying their information from policemen.

There were plenty of other rake-offs, from insurance assessors seeking early information about burglaries, from security companies and personnel officers wanting information from the Criminal Records Office, from solicitors wanting a selective reading of their clients' previous convictions.

In the Sixties corruption moved into the big time. Lowly officers in the West End divisions moved into large houses in the better suburbs and put their boys down for public schools. A posting to West End Central or the drug or vice squads became the equivalent of a winning line on the football pools. Corrupt detectives were inheriting the positions of power and were able to protect people down the line. Bribes began to be counted in 'telephone numbers', four figures or more.

The word was that detectives now went out looking for 'business' instead of letting it come to them. They made drugs raids on pop stars about to go on tour, who would pay large sums for bail, they offered protection to pornographers and were paid in advance to be somewhere else during the commission of major crime.

Whaley did not care whether the rumours were entirely true. The fact that they could circulate so openly meant that corruption had reached a level where it was part of everyday life.

His day seemed to have come when he was promoted Commander and put in charge of internal discipline. Without warning he bypassed CI, the 'Rubber Heels Squad' which, at that time, was charged with investigating complaints against policemen of criminal conduct. The custom by which an officer under suspicion was given enough warning to get rid of evidence stopped with equal abruptness. The first half dozen cases presented to him brought Whaley and a few trusted – but not too trusted – colleagues round to the suspect's station with the suddenness of a heart attack. Soon four detectives were serving prison sentences and the whole of the Metropolitan Police CID was in a carefully orchestrated uproar.

The detective hierarchy badgered the Commissioner with complaints of low morale. Fleet Street crime reporters poured out interviews with unnamed detectives who told them they could no longer meet their informants for fear they would come under suspicion of having improper dealings with criminals. MPS, to whose peccadilloes blind eyes had been turned, asked questions in the House, and the air was thick with the old claim that a policeman could always be relied upon to turn in a bent copper.

Whaley, warned to go easy, replied with half a dozen more arrests. There was a secret meeting of the Scotland Yard top brass at which he was sentenced to administrative death. His staff was 'borrowed' for important jobs and never returned; he was dropped from the circulation lists of important memoranda and reports; complaints were channelled back to the hands of CI. The loudest sound in Whaley's office, the joke went, was the ticking of the clock.

He stood it for a year then, walled up in silence, feeling betrayed, he applied for the post of Deputy Chief Constable of South Wessex Constabulary. Backed by the enthusiastic testimonials of the Met, he got the job, and when the Chief Constable died of a heart attack a few months later Whaley succeeded him. Ironically, soon after Whaley had left the Yard a new Commissioner was appointed with carte blanche to clean up the Met's Augean stables. He invited Whaley to help him, but the bitter memory of his time as the ghost of Scotland Yard caused him physical nausea whenever he had to go to that gleaming skyscraper in Victoria, and he stayed where he was.

In Pryke he recognized the archetypal CID baron of the kind who had beaten him once. He was determined to do battle again, and this time to win. But he would be patient, give Pryke plenty of rope, let him think that Whaley's time in the Met had chastened him. Sooner or later, he was confident, Pryke was sure to overreach himself. Then Whaley would move, get rid of Pryke, break up the Praetorian Guard of the CID, institute a system of cross-posting with the Uniform Branch so that a CID elite would have no chance to form.

He confided his plan to nobody. Only Dave Nicholas had some inkling of what was in Whaley's mind, and that was by deduction when he was ordered to produce statistics to show what percentage of crime was cleared up by routine procedures, luck, or assistance from the public as against classical detective methods.

So, when Whaley considered the report of the shebeen raid and the complaints against Chief Inspector Hopkins, he wondered whether this gave him the weapon he was looking for.

He dismissed the idea. If the roughing up of a few coloureds during a hunt for the killer of a policeman was used as an excuse for getting rid of the man who was leading the hunt, the sympathy would all be on Pryke's side. He decided to be as accommodating over this incident as he had been on others in the past. But Whaley had a feeling about this case. Success would be important to Pryke. Perhaps too important.

Hopkins bounced into the murder room. Just the sight of his cocksure face cheered Ritchie. If Hopkins had been in serious trouble he would have tried to conceal the fact, but Ritchie did not think he would be able to counterfeit such gaiety and confidence.

Hopkins recounted the interview with Whaley. The Chief had nodded his silver head sympathetically as Hopkins had graphically described how Black had thrown his weight around and tried to provoke a walkout, even a riot. 'We were greatly outnumbered, Sir, and firm handling was required or the situation could have got dangerously out of hand. Far from my planting cannabis on him, he showed all the signs of being under its influence. The pupils of his eyes were reduced to pinpricks and he was wild and emotional in his language. He told me I had to give him special treatment, and that he was an important man. I ordered an officer to restrain him because he was waving his arms about in an excited manner and might have hit somebody, if only by accident. The atmosphere was such that it needed only a spark to cause an explosion. The cannabis was discovered not by me but by the searching officer, and at no time did I touch him. Sgt Ritchie, who was restraining him, did not have a hand free and could not have planted anything.'

Pryke had added: 'And of course, Mr Hopkins did uncover a serious crime of violence, a stabbing now being investigated by officers not seconded to the murder squad.'

Whaley said soothingly: 'Quite so. I know how quickly things can get out of hand. Once these people acquire a dash of respectability it often goes to their heads. And as far as the people who had cannabis but were not charged are concerned, you no doubt took the view that, with a far more serious crime under investigation, charging a large number of people with what is, by comparison, a minor matter would have been a serious drain on your limited resources?'

Hopkins muttered an astonished: 'Yes, Sir,' and waited for a trap to be sprung, but Whaley merely said: 'Black has been formally charged and cautioned, so we had better let the matter stand for the moment. He is by way of being a government employee, if indirectly, and perhaps the best way to handle it is for me to have a chat with the Home Office. No doubt it will be borne in upon him that the situation was somewhat unusual and that the best way of helping race relations will be for both sides to let the matter drop.'

He added: 'This incident backs up the point of my remarks earlier today. We must not let our emotions rule us in this case.'

Hopkins muttered his assent and left Whaley and Pryke to discuss the progress of the case and administrative matters.

Hopkins did not describe all that had happened to Ritchie, but said: 'The Old Man took it like a lamb. I don't think we'll hear any more.'

'After this morning's performance?' said Ritchie, surprised. 'I thought he'd be demanding that heads roll.'

'That was just for the record,' said Hopkins, airily. 'Just to remind us not to take this bugger apart, when we get him.'

Ritchie told Hopkins about his interview with the dead man's parents and pointed to the passage in Mr James's statement about Johnson. Hopkins read it carefully. 'Time we had a chat with him. Call in Jimmy Clegg.'

Detective Sergeant Clegg was the senior half of the Ridley drug squad. He and Hopkins conferred for a few minutes about the best time and place to pick Johnson up. 'When's he most likely to have some H on him?' demanded Hopkins. 'It might help things along if we've got something to hold him on.'

'Best pull him in the evening, then,' Clegg said. 'He sleeps most of the day except when he goes to London to score, and he never keeps anything in the house a moment longer than necessary. He hides his stuff outside somewhere and just brings it in when he shoots up.'

'This evening, then,' Hopkins said.

'You want me in on it?' Ritchie asked.

Hopkins considered. 'I think we both need some rest, and I want you to do a tour of your snouts tonight. No, give this a miss. We'll call you on the radio if we need you. In the meantime, I'm going to bed and you'd better do the same.'

Five hours later, after a short sleep, a long bath, a shave and a meal had restored Ritchie to some semblance of an alert, intelligent detective, he was back in the murder room to find out if there was anything new to bear in mind before he started on his snouting expedition. He found the atmosphere tense, irritable — which was not surprising, many of the detectives having been on duty for fifteen hours on the trot — and depressed. Hopkins had not returned and Pryke had also gone home for rest. Fullalove was in charge, snapping the head off anybody who spoke to him, driving out those who were having a quiet breather between inquiries, and generally acting like a bear with a sore head.

'What's up, Ray? You look a bit frayed,' asked Ritchie.

'It's been a bloody shambles,' Fullalove said. 'That bastard Tompkins blew the story about the shebeen raid and the complaint just before we had the first Press conference this afternoon. We've got the whole Fleet Street circus baying for information. And television, as well as the locals. Pryke cocked the whole thing up by first of all trying to throw Tompkins out, then when he was persuaded not to he sat there glowering at the Press, refusing to tell them any more than they already knew.

'Whaley was there. He started it off by saying what a fine

officer James was, marked for the top and that, the usual bullshit. Then Pryke gave them the bare details, and when I say bare, I mean just that. It was as much as they could get out of him to say that James was stabbed. They got riled and one of them asked about the complaint and Pryke started shouting at them as though they were a load of schoolboys and they walked out, all of them except Tompkins who sat there with a fat grin on his face. Pryke's blaming him, of course, and he's probably right. But it's Pryke's fault as well. If he'd given them something decent to write about they wouldn't be wasting time on some nignog's complaint.'

Ritchie whistled sadly at this recital and silently cursed Tompkins for his readiness to retaliate for Pryke's taunts.

Fullalove continued: 'The hell of it is that Whaley thought he could persuade Black to drop the complaint, but now it's out in the open he may not be able to. I dunno, you wouldn't think we've got the most important murder case in the country on the go, would you?'

'You bloody wouldn't,' said Ritchie, fervently. 'What's the state of things? Anything new?'

'Not much. Door-to-door inquiries haven't turned up a lot, but they aren't completed. One woman reckons to have heard voices followed by a grunt during the night but can't pinpoint a time. Nobody else claims to have heard anything at all. Chasing up the people who left the shebeen before we raided it is tying up too many men, but we're keeping it up and widening the door-to-door effort. There's a couple of teams picking up possible suspects. We haven't ruled many people out, and who's got an alibi for that time of the morning except with wives and girlfriends? Found Fred the Greek's garage packed with those slot machines that got stolen in Bristol the other week, though.'

'Has Johnson been pulled yet?'

'Yeah. He's being worked on now. Says he was shagging his bird all night. So far she says the same thing. We took his flat apart and didn't find anything, not even heroin, so I expect he'll be released. Yeah, I've seen James's dad's statement. Christ, what a fairy that bloke was. Didn't smoke or drink or go out with lewd women. Then he gets hisself stabbed. Shows what clean living does for you. Well, better start your snouting.' Fullalove stalked off to bark at two young detectives who had returned from their meal in an offensively good humour. Ritchie winked at them and went to call on the O'Hanlon family as a prelude to a tour of the pubs.

Everybody who knew of the O'Hanlons agreed that they were a disgrace to a decent English town. Ritchie liked them. He had nicked them all at one time or another, but never with hard feelings on either side.

All were involved in prostitution, the three girls practising, their brother, Mick, and mother providing protection and housekeeping services, and living off their earnings.

Mick greeted him expansively: 'Come on in. Is it a business call, or will you take a drop?'

'I'll take a drop, unless you're foolish enough to give me a reason why I shouldn't.'

He followed Mick to the big old-fashioned kitchen where Mrs O'Hanlon sat toothless, her thighs open and stockings rolled down to her calves to reveal fish-belly white legs, veined like Stilton, welcoming him with a gruesome smile.

'Hello, Ma,' Ritchie said. 'You shouldn't have bothered to make yourself look beautiful for me.'

The crone cackled and Mick poured out a half tumbler of Irish whiskey. Ritchie said 'Slainte' and took a gulp. 'Where are the girls, working?'

'Sure.'

'Well you'll have to shut up shop now.'

'And why will that be?'

'That copper who got murdered. We don't allow that kind of thing. So there will be no naughty goings on until we catch the bloke who did it.'

'Jesus! It wasn't us. When we're nicked we go along in a quiet civilized manner.'

'I know you do. But we're clamping down so that anybody who knows anything has got a good reason for telling us.'

'And how are we going to hear anything if the girls can't work?'

'Your problem. Or I'll tell you what. The girls can work provided you report daily about what they've seen or heard.'

'Could be risky if it gets about.'

'Take it or leave it. It's either that or they stay off the streets.' He got up. 'Bye, Ma. You tell Mick to be sensible, because if he holds anything back I swear I'll drive all of you out of Ridley. I'll see myself out.'

The O'Hanlons listened until the front door slammed. The old woman hobbled over to Ritchie's barely touched glass of whiskey and sank it. 'Do as he says,' she told Mick. 'What do we care about some tearaway with a knife?'

Ritchie was pleased. Once he'd got the O'Hanlon tribe reporting daily he would see that they kept on doing so, even after this case was over.

His calls that evening took him to a cross-section of the town's criminal population – thieves, pimps, receivers, shebeen operators, conmen, lorry hijackers, dirty book dealers. He looked for signs of strain, asked after people, left messages that he wanted to hear from others. Already a number of the people he visited had been picked up for questioning. With those who were angry and hostile he dropped his veneer of friendliness and laid it on the line. Grudgingly they agreed to stay in touch.

The fact that there was no immediate feedback did not worry him. The killer would be lying low, terrified at the consequences of what was probably a panic reaction. But if he was known in the criminal milieu he could not evade suspicion for long. If he dropped out of circulation the fact would be noted and reported. Or if he was reluctant to embark upon some criminal enterprise, or if he talked too much in his cups with some trusted crony. He would have to be possessed of iron self-control not to give himself away. And when the squeeze began to bite, when money was short and the bonds of loyalty and friendship dissolved, the idea of restoring a semblance of normality by means of a short phone call to Ridley nick would become overpoweringly attractive to somebody. Ridley was not Soho. Nobody would fear a shot in the head from the killer's friends.

Always assuming of course that the killer was local and a member of the criminal population.

At four in the morning, suffering from heartburn from the numerous glasses of neat whiskey he had consumed, Ritchie rolled into bed having worked twenty-four hours in the previous thirty. His last call had been to the murder room, where he had been informed that Johnson and his bird, Alison Parker, had been released.

5

BLEARILY awake, Ritchie read the *Daily Express* and *Daily Mail* reports of the murder, spreading the papers over the breakfast table as he sipped his tea.

It was the main story in both. A picture of Rodney James had been blown up so that it seemed to occupy half the page. The *Express* headline consisted of one word in enormous type: 'KNIFED!' The *Mail* was more wordy: 'THE COWARDLY KILLER'.

Aware of the smell of whiskey and stale tobacco clinging to him, Ritchie went through the stories. 'A young policeman died in yesterday's cold dawn,' said the *Express*, 'stabbed while patrolling alone in a sleeping town.

'PC Rodney James had been in the force a bare four months before an unknown killer brought his career to an end. But already he had been marked out for the top.

'Yesterday Arthur Whaley, Chief Constable of South Wessex, was close to tears as he told me: "PC James was young, intelligent and conscientious. Had he lived he would have gone far."

'Now an unknown thug with a knife has ended a brilliant career while it was no more than a promise. But PC James's colleagues have sworn that they will not rest until the killer is brought to justice.'

Even though Ritchie's head was throbbing, he could not restrain a laugh. 'It wasn't dawn, I doubt that Whaley said that or that he was near tears, but apart from that, I can't fault it,' he told Janet.

She shrugged. 'It's what people want to read.'

61

Karen burst in, grabbing a cup of tea before leaving for college. Having a proper breakfast ran a poor second to those last few minutes in bed. 'Terrible about that young policeman. Was he as marvellous as the evening papers said?'

'If he was he'd be Chief Constable by now. The consensus is that he was a right tit, and probably a bit of a poof.'

'Didn't know you had such things in the police.'

'We don't. Especially not when they've been murdered on duty. Then they're the greatest thing since sliced bread. Speaking of which, it's about time you got up in time to have breakfast.'

Karen shuddered. 'Couldn't. I'd throw up.'

Janet looked nastily at her, then at Ritchie. 'She was out until one o'clock.'

He said casually: 'With anybody I know?'

Equally casually she said: 'I doubt it. A boy from college.'

'Oh,' said Ritchie, and went back to his paper. But it wasn't Janet's way to leave a sore unpicked.

'Some hairy yob, I suppose.' She turned on Ritchie, her mouth twisted, her voice shrewish. 'You're supposed to be her father. Do something. Or are you going to wait until she brings a little black baby home?'

Karen snatched her bag and launched herself out of the house, which shook to the slamming of the front door. Janet waited for the quarrel, but Ritchie had no stomach for it. He took the papers up to the lavatory and locked himself in, ignoring Janet's parting shot: 'You're as useless a parent as you are a policeman.'

Ritchie continued to read the papers. Neither mentioned the Press conference walkout, nor did they make much of the shebeen raid. Neither had anything about Black and his complaints, but the *Mail* mentioned the other stabbing, quoting Pryke as saying there was not thought to be a connection. They also speculated on the likelihood of the killer being a petty criminal, so either they had been doing a bit of intelligent guesswork or Pryke had been accepting their hospitality.

Half an hour later, feeling queasier than ever in the dense pall of tobacco smoke, he was back in the incident room awaiting the opening of the second day's conference. It was a long wait. Pryke was with Whaley, discussing the progress of the case.

Whaley was not happy with the way things were going. He knew word had been put round that all criminal activity must cease until the killer was found, and it reinforced his suspicions of CID. It meant that the police had it in their power to stifle organized crime at any time but chose not to do so. He had kicked up a fuss at the Yard in 1966 when the Vice Squad let it be known they intended to close down clip joints for the duration of the World Cup – it being thought undesirable that London should gain a reputation for fraudulent vice – and asked why, if they could be closed temporarily, they could not be closed permanently. Lack of manpower he was told, and he knew this would also be Pryke's reply if he broached the subject now.

Instead he turned to the Press conference debacle. Pryke defended himself with vigour. It was standard practice to control the flow of news in major cases, he pointed out. Thus the media published only that which the investigating officer – he, Pryke – wanted known.

With a slight smile, Whaley asked whether standard practice included calling news conferences and refusing to give out news. Or losing his temper.

The memory of the conference brought the blood to Pryke's face. 'It was Tompkins who ... ' he started.

Whaley cut him off with a weary gesture. 'I know all about Tompkins. Why we should be cursed with him when most freelances bend over backwards to keep in with the police, I don't know. But he's a fact of life and it's a mistake to let him needle you. Fortunately only the *Guardian* has mentioned Black's complaint, and even they have made less of it than they might have. The Press is usually suggestible in these matters, providing one sweetens the pill.'

He knew he was needling Pryke, and stopped the process

before it went too far. He did not want the killer to get away as the price of ridding himself of his head of CID. He said dismissively: 'We haven't got off to a very good start, but I suppose things can only improve.'

Pryke went straight to the murder room, where those who knew him noted the familiar signs of rage and made up their minds to keep their heads down. He went straight into a review of the events – or lack of them – of the previous twenty-four hours, distributing blame at machinegun pace. Fullalove was criticized again for not having searched roof gutters, Ritchie for not having completed background inquiries – Pryke managed to insinuate that he was trying to avoid the footslogging jobs – and Nicholas for not being up-to-date with statements. Even Hopkins got a rocket for not having checked out the ownership of all the cars parked in the street.

When question time came nobody had anything to say except Ritchie, who wanted to know whether Johnson had been ruled out.

Fullalove answered: 'Of the people we picked up yesterday only one or two have been ruled out because of positive alibis. As you would expect, most of them say they were in bed. That's what Johnson says and his bird confirms it. They say they went to bed about midnight, had sexual intercourse and went to sleep. Can't shake either of them, but if we pick up any evidence that shows he might not have been in bed, he's very much in. That also applies to everybody else of course.'

Hopkins and his team were still cross-checking the movements of people who had left the shebeen before the raid. 'Most of them say they were screwing as well. What Inspector Fullalove says about Johnson applies there.'

Pryke took over. 'That's it, then. Eighty so-called detectives chasing their tails and not one lead worth a light. Let's put some effort into it today.'

There was a smouldering silence as the squad, most of whose members had worked three quarters of the preceding twenty-four hours, left their seats to find their assignments. Detectives from all over South Wessex, many of whom had volunteered for this case, were beginning to wish they had stayed on their own patches. The fact that the squad's morale was so low on only the second day was worrying to the older hands. 'What we need,' thought Ritchie, 'is a quick break.'

Pryke's jibe that Ritchie was trying to avoid the footslogging had the force of truth. Ritchie disliked door-to-door inquiries, asking questions from a pro forma to the point where, faced with the inarticulate, you felt tempted to answer the questions for them. Besides, Ritchie thought, it was a waste of his unrivalled knowledge of the town to have him doorstepping. Against that, he did not want to be considered a shirker, so he determined to finish his background inquiries quickly and make himself available for other duties.

He made the Thomas Hardy School his first call. It had been his old school, a secondary modern whose pupils took pride in the claim that it produced the largest proportion of the town's juvenile crime. Since then it had gone comprehensive, but Ritchie still made frequent visits to the four-square Victorian edifice with its green copper pepperpot turrets. The smell of wet clothes, floor polish and school dinners took him effortlessly back a quarter of a century. He had not enjoyed school and had not joined the Old Boys' Association which his old headmaster had tried to foist upon his hostile pupils, but nostalgia for his wasted youth took him by the throat.

It was probably this which enabled a half-seen face to pluck the chords of his memory. A figure in a tatty gown darted out of a side corridor in front of him.

As though feeling Ritchie's eyes, the man looked over his shoulder. Even then it took a moment.

'Mucky?' said Ritchie incredulously. 'Mucky Alwyn?'

The man whirled round. He peered nervously at Ritchie. 'Is that Jack Ritchie?' he asked.

'None other.' Ritchie extended his hand. 'How's it going, Mucky? So you're a teacher now? I never thought when I was duffing you up in Ratty Nellie's art classes you'd be joining the other side, or I'd have thumped you harder.'

The teacher took Ritchie's hand gingerly. 'I wish you wouldn't call me that. I thought I'd lived it down. If any of the children hear it, I'll never be called anything else.'

Ritchie grinned and nodded. The nickname had nothing to do with Alwyn Sendle's personal hygiene. He had always been rather fastidious. It had first been applied to him in his third year, when he was found in flagrante delicto in a school lavatory with another boy. Although the incident had resulted in a ferocious public beating for both of them and the nickname which stuck with Sendle for the rest of his schooldays, the school had not regarded the episode with any great horror, most of them having indulged in similar experiences. Even Ritchie, aggressively heterosexual though he was, had once allowed himself to be kissed by another boy – the one Sendle was caught with, as a matter of fact – but had found the experience unerotic and had not repeated it.

There was a moment's pause before Sendle, who seemed ill at ease, said: 'You haven't changed too much. Do you still live in Ridley? I moved north and came back a couple of years ago. What do you do?'

The light was poor, but did a flicker of fear cross Sendle's face when Ritchie replied that he was a detective? If so, Sendle's voice betrayed nothing.

'Why are you here? Is it about poor Rodney James?'

'Yes. Did you know him?'

'A little. He used to come to my extra music classes. A nice boy. No gift, you understand, but he tried to understand and his interest was not confined to the latest pop group. I find today's pop even more meaningless than when we were young.'

They came to a better lit area and Ritchie took a closer look at Sendle. Twenty-five years had sat heavily upon him. Perhaps

Sendle was thinking the same of him, but Ritchie knew that he did not have the same defeated look that time had etched on the teacher's monkeylike features, nor the red-rimmed eyes. Even his clothing had gone to seed, although there was a hint of his former dapperness in his waisted jacket and large bow-tie. But his check shirt had had at least one full day's wear since its last wash. On the other hand, he had not run to fat and he looked little heavier than in the days when he had been a respectable athlete.

There was defensiveness in Sendle's counter-appraisal, as though he knew what Ritchie was thinking and wanted not to care.

'Is there anything else I can tell you? I'm not sure I can be of much use. Rodney was not in my form, you know.'

'Rodney? Do masters call boys by their first names these days?'

'Senior boys, yes, if we want to. We try to treat them as equals, to understand them, rather than trying to rule by fear. That incident with me ... you know, when I got that nickname, it wouldn't happen like that now. We would realize that such an incident might be almost meaningless, and if not, should be treated by properly qualified help. Not by beating a boy in front of the whole school.'

For the first time Ritchie realized how much that incident, which had seemed such a joke, must have scarred Sendle. Perhaps it was the first time he had brought himself to talk about it. That nickname, which he had wanted so much to forget, must have turned a key in his memory and opened a long-closed door.

Ritchie felt embarrassed. During the course of his work a policeman sees all sides of human sexuality. He enforced the law without the censoriousness that many of his colleagues brought to the task. 'Show me the man whose sex life contains nothing he would rather hide, and I'll show you a corpse,' he used to say during canteen discussions of some sex offence.

He wanted to get away from Sendle without seeming brusque. 'We must keep in touch,' he said.

'I don't think so,' said Sendle disconcertingly. 'I thought you a rather brutal youth and I cannot imagine our interests have grown any closer over the years. Still,' he added kindly, 'it was nice of you to suggest it.'

Ritchie laughed, unembarrassed at having his small hypocrisy laid bare. 'OK, Alwyn, direct me to Mr Clarke, would you? And perhaps we'll meet again in another twenty-five years. We'll be collecting our pensions then. How's that for a thought?'

He was still smiling when he found Clarke's classroom on the second floor and introduced himself to the short fat history teacher who had been James's last form master.

'A terrible thing,' he said. 'An awful thing. You know, I was most surprised to hear that James had gone into the police. Such a coarse profession, as I've always understood it. Necessary, no doubt, and I've always had the greatest admiration for people in your work, but not the sort of job for a sensitive person. We had an officer here once to give us a lecture about drugs, and the things he said and the pictures he showed us made me feel quite ill. He didn't turn a hair, of course. Nor did the boys, come to that. I heard them match their experiences against what he had said and come to the conclusion he didn't know what he was talking about.'

Despite his impatience, Ritchie chuckled. Jimmy Clegg's lecture on drugs was highly popular despite – or, more probably, because of – its grisly horrors. It went down a treat with the Women's Institute and the Townswomen's Guild. He would enjoy telling him that the kids at whom it was aimed took it with a sackful of salt.

On the subject of James, Clarke had little more to say than Mr James, Marylin, or even Mucky Alwyn. It was the same picture of a quiet, unassertive youth who gave no trouble and had no friends other than Desmond Hagley. He had won some honours at school sports, and some academic prizes. He had been a prefect but fell short of the leadership qualities required for head boy.

Ritchie left the subject of James and asked Clarke if he knew

Ralph Johnson. The teacher's open, slightly weak face clouded over. 'Do I not? I rarely describe boys as evil, but he surely was. He came from a good home and his younger brother was completely different. But Johnson was dishonest, cruel and ruthless. He had been expelled from at least three schools and he was expelled from here. Demanding money with menaces, I think you would call it. He beat up a younger boy, James's friend Hagley, as a matter of fact, and took his dinner money.'

'Hagley? Not James?'

'I'm sure it wasn't. The head might be able to confirm it. Why, is Johnson mixed up in this?'

'We're looking into all possibilities. This is one of many. We have to check on everybody James might have had dealings with and eliminate them if possible. So don't jump to conclusions about Johnson. We're looking at him along with a couple of hundred others.'

Clarke did not seem to have heard. 'I could believe anything of Johnson,' he said. 'Including murder.'

Despite his off-hand reaction to Clarke's question, Ritchie's interest in Johnson was now intense. In crime investigation a name might crop up several times for no apparent reason. There may not be anything positive to link the person with the crime but often the connection is there. As Ritchie drove back to the police station with Clarke's statement he was regretting that Johnson had already been pulled in and released. He could be picked up again at any time, of course, but the element of surprise had been lost.

Like every other copper in Ridley, Ritchie knew Johnson and loathed him. He had put him away twice. Johnson had been a drug pusher with Capone-sized ambitions. He had worked at providing himself with a monopoly in Ridley by frightening off the opposition with violence. Those who wouldn't be frightened he stitched up, his favourite method being to sell an opponent some drugs, then inform on him to the police.

After he had gained a clear field he began to extend his

customers by turning on youngsters, particularly young girls who had left home after rows with their parents, and who would then become a source of income and sex.

One day Ritchie and another detective had raided Johnson's flat. They found no drugs, for he knew better than to keep them at home. But Ritchie found a decaying leather jacket, which he seized and sent off to the police forensic laboratories at Cardiff. Inside a rip in the lining was found the faintest trace of heroin powder. It was enough, and Johnson received his first sentence for possession. It was a short one, and within a few months Johnson was back in Ridley reclaiming his market.

But by now he had been marked down. One day Ritchie took a call from the Yard's drug squad that Johnson had been seen in Soho with a large-scale pusher but had evaded arrest. Ritchie had acted rapidly. With another detective he staked out Ridley station. They had nabbed Johnson with a big enough haul of different narcotics to mark him down as a major pusher. Knowing he faced a long sentence, Johnson had tried to kick his way clear. All he gained was some bruises and a conviction for assaulting the police to add to his form.

Since he had returned to Ridley after his last sentence he was no longer the force he had once been. He knew he could not risk large-scale dealing, and anyway the scene had shifted, become more amorphous. The users bought their supplies in from London or Bristol on a cooperative basis. Johnson began to prey on the drug milieu in a different way, stealing their dope and money by threat of violence.

Ridley CID noted his deterioration. He became known as 'Toe-Rag' Johnson. Toe-Rag is the epithet police apply to the dregs — flashers, people who steal from pensioners or church collection boxes. The epithet had been applied to Johnson so often and with such disgust that it became part of his name.

Ridley police kept an eye on him and waited for one of his victims to inform on him so that they could put him away again.

6

BARELY had Ritchie put his nose into the murder room than he sensed a new and charged atmosphere.

'This could be it,' said Dave Nicholas, having listened impatiently to Ritchie's report of his conversation with Clarke. 'Just round the corner, in Mafeking Avenue, there's this old lady, bedridden, nothing to do but watch the world go by from her window. She was missed first time round because the doctor said she wasn't fit to be interviewed.

'Anyway, today she was seen by Gotobed. "Oh," she says, "when nobody came to see me I thought my information couldn't be any use."

"What information is this?" asks Gotobed.

"The car, of course," she says, as though Gotobed was an idiot. "The two people in the car when the policeman was killed. Isn't it important?"

'Finally Gotobed realizes she thinks that we're mind readers. He got a statement off her. Apparently she couldn't sleep because she'd got heartburn. She heard this car drive up in the middle of the night. Her bed is right by the window so she looks out and sees a white car turn into a drive that leads to a row of garages and nowhere else, but nobody came out.

'She dozed off but she got woken up by a train stopping on the embankment. That was about an hour after the car arrived. She knows because she checked whether it was time to take some pills. A few minutes later the car leaves with two people in it. We've checked and none of the garage owners have white cars.'

'So what?' said Ritchie. 'A couple having it off in a nice quiet spot. Used to do it myself in my evil youth. Never killed a copper though.'

'Maybe. But mark the time. Grannie says they went in shortly before two o'clock and left about three – that was about the time James got his – and, she says, in a hell of a hurry.

'It wouldn't be the first time somebody got killed through surprising a couple on the job. People do get very bad-tempered when they're interrupted on the vinegar strokes.'

'Except that they were at it – *if* they were at it – in Mafeking Avenue and our hero was found dead in Kimberley Road.'

'Pryke thinks the body could have been dumped there to confuse us.'

Ritchie burst into laughter. 'If they were just an innocent couple up to nothing more serious than a bit of how's your father they're going to have a job convincing us. Well, it'll teach them to enjoy themselves.'

However cynical Ritchie felt about the value of this new lead, Pryke was throwing all his weight behind it. Bustling in from his private office he saw Ritchie with a copy of the old woman's statement. 'Read yourself in on that,' he said. 'She caught a bit of a registration number and we're having a check done and interviewing all the possibles as they come in.'

Nicholas had summed up the statement neatly enough. The car was white, looked new and expensive. She remembered a bit of the number because the second and third letters were DF, which were her son's initials. She thought there was a 5 in the remainder of the number.

An additional statement said she had been shown pictures of different makes of car and thought the vehicle she had seen might be a Rover 2000 or 3.5, a Triumph 2000 or 2.5, or a Ford Escort or a BMW.

'That's fine,' Ritchie told Gotobed. 'They've all got three things in common, an engine, a wheel at each corner, and windscreen wipers. What could be simpler?'

Nettled, Gotobed said: 'It's the only lead anybody's come up with. If you've got a better hole, go to it.'

'I haven't. I'll settle for yours.'

A vehicle check is a laborious operation. First the squad had to trace all the people in the town who owned white cars with DF numberplates. Then the search spread outwards through the county, the region and, maybe, the whole country until thousands of people had received visits from polite young men 'from the murder squad' asking if they could account for their movements at the time in question.

Allowance had to be made for other possibilities: that the colour of the car had been changed without the logbook being amended, or that the car was not one of the types specified by the witness, or that the car was not white but yellow or a very light pastel shade of green or blue which might look white in artificial light, or that the registration letters were not DF at all, but OF.

Pryke, against Hopkins' advice, did not put out an immediate release to Press and television reporters asking for public assistance. He preferred to see if the squad could turn up the vehicle on its own. Three days had gone by, and reporters were beginning to shift back to London, before he grudgingly consented to put out a call for the assistance of the public. As was inevitable with such vague information, a deluge of calls resulted, all of which had to be checked by a squad which was beginning to feel that it was battering its way through cotton wool.

A week after the murder the television station covering the south of England put on a special presentation during the regional news. The old lady was interviewed and described the car to the best of her ability. Pictures of her 'possibles' were flashed on to the screen together with letters and figures she remembered from the numberplate. The phone number of Ridley police station was shown and read out.

Two items later there was a report on a crisis in dairy farming and Mr Martin Tilt, MP for the neighbouring constituency of White Horse Vale, was shown demonstrating his concern by driving round farms in his constituency, accompanied by television cameras, for carefully staged discussions over the backs of cows specially cleaned up for the occasion.

Within minutes the lines of Ridley police station were being jammed with callers pointing out that Tilt's car was a white Rover and that the registration was HDF 65 S.

A swift check revealed that the car had not long been in Tilt's hands and was not yet registered in his name. Ritchie and Gotobed were dispatched to the red brick Regency house which snuggled in a vale on Salisbury Plain, where the MP lived when not attending Parliament.

Although they had phoned and been told that Tilt was expected, he had not got back by the time they arrived. They were entertained by Mrs Tilt, a handsome woman in her late forties. She guessed what it was about, having seen the programme and noticed the coincidence, but it was nonsense, of course. There had been a late sitting at the House that night so her husband could not possibly have been killing policemen in the back streets of Ridley.

Martin Tilt arrived, looking strained and angry. 'I don't blame you,' he said. 'I blame those television people. You would think that with all their resources they could prevent this kind of thing happening.'

Ritchie, who privately found the situation comic, nodded with a straight face.

'Oh, surely, it's nothing to be upset about. A chance in a million,' said Mrs Tilt soothingly. 'I've told these officers, and all the Press who have called, that you were attending a late sitting and couldn't have been anywhere near Ridley.'

'Pressmen?' yelped Tilt. 'Oh my God.'

Ritchie wondered why he was so upset. As Mrs Tilt had said, surely it was no more than coincidence. He asked what kept Tilt at the House that night.

'Oh, the Industrial Development Bill. A three-line whip,' Tilt muttered as he led them to another room so that they could take a statement.

He poured drinks. 'None of that duty nonsense,' he said, and drained his. He drew a deep breath. 'Look, you might as well know, that was my car. I wasn't at the House. There wasn't an all-night sitting. I was with my secretary, who comes from Ridley, and I was just dropping her home. We stopped for ... well, you know,' and his voice tailed off miserably.

'Sexual intercourse, sir?' said Ritchie, bluntly.

'Yes,' said Tilt, violently. 'Sexual intercourse, a bit of grumble, a lay, a fuck. It's bad enough having to tell you, but there'll be hell to pay if the Press says I was at the House. I shall have to tell my wife. Christ, what a mess!'

Ritchie could sympathize. It was like having it off in the middle of a field. Suddenly floodlights come on and you find you're performing in the middle of Wembley Stadium. He took a statement. 'We'll have to see the girl, er, Miss Briant,' he said. 'But as far as we're concerned it will remain confidential.'

Tilt snorted. 'Confidential to you and anybody who reads a newspaper. Well, I'd better tell my wife and get it over with, I suppose.'

As they turned their car in the drive they could see a tableau in the drawing room, Mrs Tilt seated, Tilt standing, grief and humiliation in his face.

'Could he have done it?' wondered Gotobed. 'He's got a lot to lose.'

'Like what? If he was Prime Minister, maybe, but obscure backbenchers don't resign over sex scandals, not as long as they are hetero, anyway. And do you suppose he carries a flick-knife for emergencies?'

Gotobed shrugged. 'We'd better see the girl, though. If she tells the same story I can at least put her down in my little black book. You can't know enough confirmed goers.'

Katharine Briant proved more reluctant than Tilt to admit anything. 'He just gave me a lift home,' she said stubbornly. 'The only reason we stopped was because he wanted to make sure he had given me certain order papers.'

She stuck to her story until Gotobed sighed and said: 'Look love, don't be shy because we've heard it all before. Just tell us whether he was fucking you. It's all we need to know.'

She swallowed, taken aback by Gotobed's crudity. 'All right, yes, if you must know,' she muttered, and gave no further trouble as they took her through the events of the night. Her story confirmed Tilt's in all details.

Pryke sucked his teeth. 'If Tilt did it, they must have carted the body round the corner in the car, so all we need is a forensic examination of that. Better go through the motions,' he said, and went into his office to contemplate the likelihood of an unpleasant interview with Whaley next day.

This time his expectations were to be fulfilled. Whaley's normally tidy desk was covered with the morning newspapers. He read out headlines: ' "MP interviewed in PC murder hunt", "MP quizzed by murder squad", "TV programme lands MP in murder hunt", and they all comment on this "ghost" sitting,' he said. 'Tilt and Briant have got their pictures splashed all over the front pages. And that's not the worst. Read this poison.'

He passed over the diary page of a tabloid paper. Pryke read the story under the headline 'Tilt shaken':

'I sympathize with Martin Tilt, Conservative MP for White Horse Vale, in the misfortune which attended his late-night sitting in Ridley, which coincided with the tragic murder of a young PC.

'Mr Tilt was driving home his House of Commons secretary, vivacious Miss Katharine Briant, who lives in Ridley, when they stopped for certain policy discussions near the scene of the murder, at about the time it occurred. Police have, of course, cleared both of them.

'Miss Briant is a popular figure in the House, as indeed is Mr Tilt. Hers is a friendly personality and she is much in demand by

MPs. She was formerly a close friend of Mr Michael Hagerty, briefly under-secretary of something-or-other in one of the more obscure Ministries.'

'Ouch,' said Pryke.

'Yes,' said Whaley. 'I think "Ouch" is about right.'

'There were pressmen about when we brought Tilt's car in. I wish I knew who was leaking stuff to them.'

'Probably nobody in this case. An MP caught in a compromising situation is a much more interesting story than a policeman giving up his life for the community. I expect every paper in Fleet Street was working on it.'

'The bastards,' said Pryke.

Whaley's eyebrows rose. Pryke with a sense of moral outrage was a new thought for him.

He threw down a paper, rose and turned to the window as he always did before an unpleasant interview. It was his way of providing a punctuation mark. Pryke noticed it and braced himself.

Whaley returned to his seat and leaned back reflectively for a moment before starting to speak decisively:

'I cannot disguise my opinion that this operation has not been well handled. It is an important case for many reasons, for the sake of our and the public's morale and to demonstrate to us and to them as well as to the criminal element that we have the power and will to protect our own.

'The murder of a policeman is also a matter of national importance. The eyes of the country are upon us, and I stressed from the start the need to be seen to have run an impeccable investigation. It cannot be said that we have succeeded. A shambles would be a better description.'

Pryke, his face red, started to speak, but Whaley shut him up.

'A shambles,' he said. 'First there was that business over the shebeen. I ignored that, putting it down to the heat of the moment. On the same day there was the altercation with Tompkins. I know he is a nasty character, but you are head of

CID and you should be able to handle such people. Then, I understand, you accused several of your officers of leaking stuff to him. An unnecessary accusation, I would have thought, in view of the fact that half the town must have known about it by then. The point is, it could not have done much for morale among your own men.

'Then there was the debacle of the Press conference, which I personally found deeply embarrassing. And now this. Look at the coverage of this case. Allegations of assaults on coloured people, planting of drugs, a public walkout of the Press and now the whole thing reduced to a sordid affair between an MP and his secretary. The fact that a police officer was stabbed to death is only mentioned in passing in most papers these days.'

Pryke forced himself to remain silent and listen.

Whaley continued with his tongue-lashing: 'Clearly we are not responsible for the publicity given to Tilt, but it is the last of a series of disasters. When I am asked what the devil is happening I find it very difficult to answer. I regret now not having called in the Yard in the first place. Late as it is, and however unpleasant the repercussions may be, I am thinking of calling them in now. We have to take some steps to impose ourselves on events instead of allowing ourselves to be carried along, willy-nilly.'

Pryke could not restrain himself. He knew that the reaction of the Yard to being called in after a week would be scathing. The Yard's murder squad would leak it to the Press that they were to be made the whipping boys for the local force's failure.

'Sir,' he ground out, 'you are making me a scapegoat. This is one of the most difficult investigations I have ever been involved in. There are virtually no leads, and there would still be no leads if every detective in the world was called in. And if the Press seize on irrelevancies because we can't give them sensation, that's not my fault.'

'You miss the point,' Whaley said in a hard voice. 'I am only interested in what the Press says insofar as it seems to reflect the reality that this case has not been kept under proper control.

'In a few days' time I will be giving a report on this case to the chairman of the Police Authority. Unless there is some forward movement by then I can expect serious criticism – criticism it will be difficult for me to answer – that by not calling in the Yard we failed to bring the maximum strength to bear on this case. However, I will put the question of calling in the Yard in abeyance for the time being. Dissension between them and us would soon become public knowledge. Somewhere the killer is laughing at us already. I have no desire to give him further cause for mirth.

'If there is no progress by the time I am due to meet the chairman I shall review my decision. In any case, it is my intention to hold an official inquiry into this case after it is over, if it ever is. We may as well gain what profit we can from it. Thank you, Mr Pryke.'

His voice was dismissive. Pryke left, aware that suddenly his career was resting on a knife-edge.

Pryke had travelled the same route as Whaley, if for the opposite reason. When he heard reports of huge bribes being paid to the more unscrupulous Met detectives he would recall how his progress had been cut short by a fiver accepted from a young man of good family in return for ignoring the small amount of cannabis he had on his person. Pryke, pocketing the note, thought no more about the incident until he had an interview with the Detective Chief Inspector at his station.

The Guv'nor passed over a note from CI – at that time in charge of investigations against the police – which alleged that Pryke had accepted the bribe. 'I've been asked to investigate this. I'm very tucked up at the moment, so I shan't be able to get round to it for some time. When I do, I want you either out of this force or with a very good story.'

Pryke discovered that, a few days after he had accepted the bribe, the young man of good family had been careless enough to get caught again. This time the arresting officer was a young uniformed officer of strict religious principle, and when he proffered the bribe the young principled officer added that to the charge of possession of cannabis. The cannabis-taker panicked and tried to talk his way out by threatening to reveal that a detective had accepted a bribe. The policeman took a statement and sent it to the Yard.

Pryke could have relied on stout denial, and might have got away with it. Instead he transferred to South Wessex Constabulary with the rank of Detective Inspector and the papers in the other matter were quietly 'lost'.

Although Pryke's new basic pay was higher, he lost out considerably in allowances and expenses, not to mention those little sweeteners which came his way.

On the other hand promotion looked surer, especially after Pryke came to the Chief Constable's notice as a result of a fortunate chance while he was still unknown in the area. A thief had had the gall to break into the home of the chairman of the Police Authority and steal his valuable stamp collection. Pryke was boozing in an off-the-beaten-track pub when he heard a farm labourer asking a friend if he knew how to dispose of stamps.

Pryke was one pace behind him when he left, and outside the door the labourer found himself in an armlock. A little knee and head work elicited a confession and the whereabouts of the album. Ten minutes later Pryke had recovered it, capping his exploit with the arrest of two other men involved.

He took the album direct to the Chief Constable – bypassing his immediate superior, whom Pryke had long classified as 'that bloody swede'. After the men had been convicted, the Chief arranged a pleasant little ceremony in which Pryke personally returned the album to its owner, modestly grunting: 'Informants and routine, Sir,' when asked how he had cleared the case up.

The Chief found his rough diamond from the Met utterly fascinating, and occasionally enjoyed an evening's drinking with him, in the course of which Pryke would have cryptic conversations with people he would afterwards describe as 'one of my best snouts' or 'the smoothest conman between London and Bristol'. The Chief found it awfully interesting and never caught the look of derision on Pryke's face because Pryke took good care that he never would.

Promotion followed much more quickly than it would have done in the Met and, although Pryke calculated that if he became Chief Constable he would not make as much money as he would as a sergeant in one of the more profitable London divisions, he was not dissatisfied. He avoided any incidents such as the one that had caused his exile in the first place, and when the head of CID retired Pryke was named as his successor, to the disgust of the retiring Guv'nor, who had long previously summed up Pryke and who took his retirement gift muttering: '*Après moi, le déluge,*' or words to that effect.

Pryke started building his iron guard. Power to promote did not rest solely with him, but his recommendation was crucial. Good reports were earned by being accepted into Pryke's drinking circle, by knowing to the inch how far to go with him, and by accepting occasional turns as the butt of his malicious tongue.

Whaley's promotion after the sudden death of the old Chief had caused flutterings in the CID dovecote. His reputation as a foe of CID was well known, and although he had not moved against the CID during his period as deputy, there was speculation that he might do so now.

When the shake-up failed to materialize, the CID drew the conclusion they were expected to draw. 'He's learned not to bugger about with CID,' said Hopkins, cock-a-hoop after some stroke of Pryke's, to a sceptical Dave Nicholas.

Until this case, Pryke had thought the same. He held the reins of power so tight in his grasp that he had allowed the thought to seep into his mind that he was invulnerable.

Now this carefully constructed position was threatened. Pryke had no need to ask himself how an inquiry would view the case.

Only one thing could save him, and that was a body in the cells. Somebody had to be got for this job, and quickly.

PART TWO

7

A FEW nights later another crime took place in Ridley. The incident began when the London train drew in. A tall, ill-coordinated youth in jeans and a tightly buttoned simulated leather jacket which did not reach high enough to conceal a huge, purpling love-bite on his neck, strolled warily out of the station. His eyes, darting ceaselessly around the booking hall, belied his casual manner. What he saw gave him almost as much of a shock as would the sight of a dozen policemen meaningfully jingling their handcuffs.

He walked with a fast shambling gait through the station car park. He hardly needed to turn his head to know he was being followed. Out of the pool of light cast by the station he broke into a run, dodging the cars of the home-going commuters, heading for the black haven of the allotments.

He dived through a gap in the fence and pounded down a path for twenty yards before swerving off to lie panting behind a shed. For half an hour he listened to the rasp of his breath and felt the cold eat into his bones.

Eventually he felt reassured. After a moment's indecision he returned to the car park. He stayed on the allotment side of the fence until, satisfied nothing was moving, he crawled back through the gap.

'Wrong again, Wally,' said an iron voice in his ear, and a thudding blow to his face sent him sprawling. Recovering his scrambled wits he looked fearfully up at the assailant silhouetted against the night sky.

'Been to London to score, haven't you? Give.'

'I haven't. Straight up, I was looking for work,' said Wally.

'Work? All you can do is wank. Give me what you've got unless you want your head kicked in. Come on, give, give.' His words were reinforced by short, heavy kicks in Wally's ribs.

Wally cried out in pain and tried to curl into a ball. He slid a reluctant hand into the interior of his windcheater and found an envelope. He tried to open it to slide out some of the contents before handing it over, but it was sealed. His attacker guessed the purpose of the movement and slapped him sharply across the face, where a bruise was already beginning to swell. He jerked Wally's hand out and snatched the envelope.

'Stupid bastard,' he said tonelessly. He felt the envelope between his fingers and sensed the tiny pills inside. Pocketing the envelope he demanded: 'Got any bread on you?'

'You're joking. That score took everything I'd got. Look, give me a couple of grain. Enough for tonight. You've got ten grain there, you can spare two.'

'What do you think this is, charity week?' jeered the other, and with a parting kick in Wally's ribs walked briskly away, swinging a tightly rolled umbrella.

An observer would have been hard-put to place him. His hair was neatly cut and combed, he wore a dark-blue overcoat of good quality and fit. The retaining band of the umbrella looked like gold. Thus far he might be a young executive, a bit too short on dress sense to realize that the formality of umbrella and fitted overcoat do not go with hairy tweeds, which was what he was wearing underneath.

Closer examination would have picked up other incongruities. The shoes, though clean, were so far down at heel that their condition was beyond mere carelessness. They also seemed not to fit, and his feet slapped as he walked. The cuffs of his trousers fell too far over his shoes and were fraying. His shirt was of cheap, greying translucent nylon. There was something tough and wary in his face. Dressed differently you might put him down as a soldier in one of the tougher units, perhaps a paratrooper.

The explanation, though, was simple enough. All the clothes Ralph Johnson stood up in were stolen, except for the shirt which he had bought from an Indian market trader.

Once out of the station area, Johnson looked round carefully before melting into the ill-lit side-streets.

Ten minutes later Wally reappeared and set off towards the town centre. He sobbed occasionally, and sniffed, wiping his nose with his sleeve. Every few seconds his fingertips went tenderly to the bruise on his cheek. He turned into an Arcade and looked through the window of an espresso bar which might have been designed to catch an anticipated wave of Fifties nostalgia but had merely remained unchanged since that era.

Through the window Wally saw a group of youths and a girl sitting round a table talking to two older men. At the sight of these Wally swore and retreated to a doorway into which he huddled. He was used to waiting. It was almost his only talent. He had waited in courts, in probation offices, in remand cells, in labour exchanges, drug dependency clinics, in cafes and, the longest waits of all, on street corners or in amusement arcades waiting for his connection to turn up. If he had developed no other skill in his short, empty life, Wally knew how to wait.

This time he did not have to wait long. After twenty minutes Detective Sergeant Jimmy Clegg, head of Ridley's two-man drug squad, and his assistant, Temporary Detective Constable Bert Ambrose, left the cafe and moved up the Arcade in the opposite direction.

As soon as they disappeared Wally entered the cafe. The dispirited group, who were the only customers, brightened at the sight of him.

'Have you got the stuff?' asked the girl urgently.

Wally sat, his head bowed. He shook it wearily.

'The money then?'

Another shake. 'Johnson jumped me at the station. He was waiting for me. What fucker told him I was going to London?'

He got no answer except a groan of despair. He told his story, exaggerating the fight he put up in defence of their interests. 'He took it all,' he ended. 'Ten fucking grain.'

'Oh, Christ,' wailed a boy who looked about sixteen. He was almost weeping. 'What can we do?'

'Somebody else can make the next buy,' said Wally. 'I've had enough.'

The girl looked at him angrily. 'How do we know you were jumped? How do we know you haven't kept the stuff?'

For answer Wally showed her his bruised cheek and hauled up his shirt and revealed the red blotches round his ribs where Johnson's boot had gone in. There was a silence.

'What did Clegg want?' asked Wally to break it.

'Same as before,' he was told. 'That fucking copper what got done. Wanted to know had we heard anything. Same old shit. Keep our ears open. Don't try to protect anybody. What about Johnson? Was he still carrying a knife? They still seem to think it might have been him. Pity Clegg wasn't done in as well.'

'Pity it wasn't Johnson. I'd turn him in like a shot myself,' said Wally feelingly. Suddenly something plucked a chord in his memory. He sat motionless for a second, his eyes bright. They dulled again.

'What's about?' he asked. 'Methadone, Speed, Mandies?'

The group shrugged, almost in unison. 'There's nothing. The law is clamping down. Nobody fancies being caught bringing stuff in.'

'What about doing over a chemist?' There was no answer. The loss of the supply they had been anticipating from Wally appeared to have paralysed them. Wally got up. 'If there's nothing doing, I'm going.'

'What about the money?' demanded the sixteen-year-old. 'I only got it by thieving from me Mum's rent tin.'

'Same as a bust. I do the running, but if the law grabs me you've had your lot. Same with Johnson. Anyway, I've got no money. Anybody know where Clegg went? I don't want to run into him.'

'Probably the Red Lion,' said the girl.

In the hierarchy of drug use, the Red Lion was the haunt of cannabis users, mainly young middle-class, many of them students. Users of hard drugs rarely used it, partly out of contempt for the shit-heads, partly because money spent in pubs would be better employed buying heroin, rent or food. Wally was almost unrecognized in the dimly-lit saloon bar.

One who did notice him was TDC Ambrose, who nudged Clegg and pointed with his chin. Clegg's eyes narrowed. 'Don't usually see him here. Wonder what's up?'

They watched him from their position at the bar, but Wally did not seem to have come to talk to anybody. He felt round in his pocket for the old oilskin tobacco pouch which served him as a purse, counted out a few copper coins and went to the bar, near the detectives. 'How much is a half-pint of bitter?'

'Thirteen pee,' the barman said contemptuously. Wally checked the money in his hand, then rooted around in his pocket. Clegg came over.

'God, it's too pathetic,' he said. 'I'll get it. Half a pint of ordinary?'

Wally turned. 'Oh, if you're buying, Mr Clegg, I'll have a Scotch.'

'Don't take liberties. Half of bitter it is.'

Clegg waited until the barman had handed over the drink and moved away.

'What brings you here?'

'Thought I'd see how the other half lives.'

'Come and join us. My mate's over there.'

'No, thanks all the same, Mr Clegg. I've got a reputation to worry about. But I'll tell you what, if your car is in the market place tomorrow and you're in it I might come over for a chat. Say about noon?'

'Got something for me, then?'

'Just a chat, Mr Clegg. Oh, and Mr Clegg ... '

'Yes, Wally?'

'Bring some readies with you.' He swallowed his drink and left without looking at the detective again.

Clegg went back to Ambrose.

'What was that about?'

'Hinted he'd got something for me. Something worth money. We made a meet for tomorrow.'

'Does he do a bit of snouting?'

'Only for money.'

'Sounds like it's worth a go.'

'Yes,' said Clegg. 'It's worth a go.'

Another fifteen minutes found Wally in an empty, boarded-up house, which he had entered by a gap where a sheet of plywood had been jaggedly broken. Once in he stood for a moment, listening carefully for dossers or meths-drinkers. The latter, particularly, could be dangerous, given to bouts of murderous rage when they would fight until they could no longer stand, oblivious to pain or mercy. But the house was silent.

Lighting the way with matches, he went cautiously up the treadless stairs. At the second before the top Wally groped underneath. His hand came up with a small packet and he left the way he had come.

He walked a short distance to an old Victorian villa which was let off in rooms. It had almost the atmosphere of a commune, with men and women pairing off or separating as the fancy took them. The offspring of these or previous liaisons were looked upon as communal responsibility. Most individual property was almost valueless and borrowed and returned casually, but it was considered unneighbourly to steal anything a resident really valued.

Wally had a small room, furnished with a grubby bed, a sink and a food-encrusted Baby Belling, at the top of the house. On his way up he popped into several rooms until he found somebody who would let him have a small amount of cannabis.

The contents of the packet he had taken from the empty house seemed to be burning in Wally's pocket. He made tea, smoked a cigarette and tried to forget it. It was no use. Although he had already shot up that day, in the lavatories of St Pancras Station, he ached for more. What he had in his pocket was his emergency supply, the equivalent of the ten-pound note that some careful people keep in the back of their wallets.

He knew, without looking, how many tablets there were in the packet. Three. Wouldn't two be enough?

He took out one tablet, dissolved it in warm water and drew it into the syringe. He tied a tie tight round his upper arm to make the vein in the hollow of his elbow stand proud, then finally injected himself, intoxicated by the sight of the needle sliding into his arm, even before the drug hit the bloodstream. When it did, he felt a warmth flowing through his body, as each vein seemed to be an identifiably separate stream of sensation.

He settled down to wait for morning.

8

CLEGG arrived late, and Wally cursed him. He felt too bloody conspicuous standing among the cars under the eye of an attendant who clearly suspected him of being up to no good. When the blue CID car arrived he looked carefully in the back before joining Clegg in the front. Clegg wrinkled his nose. Wally smiled. He put his nose to the armpit of his jersey and sniffed. 'I do smell a bit,' he admitted.

'I had a dog smelled sweeter than you, but I had it put down.'

'I'll buy some washing powder when I've got some spare bread.'

'Only powder you'd buy wouldn't make any suds. And for Christ's sake, stop stirring the air,' Clegg said as Wally scratched himself. 'Incidentally, who thumped you in the face?'

Wally considered. Would telling Clegg the truth make his story more plausible by showing he had a reason to grass? Or would Clegg suspect he was trying to set Johnson up in revenge? He decided on caution: 'Fell and hit myself on a doorhandle.'

'Vicious things, doorhandles. Well, it's been lovely meeting you. I've got to go and fumigate the car now.'

'What a shame.' Wally reached for the door. 'It's been a lovely chat.'

Clegg gave in. 'Stop playing games. What's it all about?'

'Have you brought the readies?'

'We'll see about that after you've talked about whatever it is we were going to talk about.'

'We're going to talk about Toe-Rag Johnson and the late PC James who, if the papers do not lie, was a very wonderful man.

What else have you been asking about for the last couple of weeks?'

Clegg turned a stony face to the youth. 'You'd better not be joking,' he said dangerously.

Wally quailed. He had crossed the point of no return. 'I'm not playing games. I don't even know if this is any good to you. It's just something I remembered the other day and thought I ought to tell you.'

'Very public-spirited. Well, what is it?'

'At one time, before his last stretch, Johnson used to hide some of his stuff in Kimberley Road. You remember how he used to work? Made a meet, took the money, went away and came back with the stuff? I scored off him once. He made the meet in Mafeking Avenue and went round the corner. I had a look but he'd disappeared. A minute later he came out of one of those alleyways by the sides of the houses.'

'Which one?'

'I couldn't stop to see, could I? I had to scarper back to where he left me. If he'd have found me snooping he would've duffed me up, wouldn't he?'

'Well, about how far up?'

'Six or eight houses, maybe. It's a long time ago.'

'Why haven't you told me this before?'

'Christ, I didn't think about it. It was a long time ago, like I said. Maybe three or four years. It was only the other day it clicked, when I was in that area, in a road with the same sort of houses.'

'Which road was this?' Clegg asked, sharply.

'Balaclava, I think.'

Clegg looked at Wally, not happy with this sudden inspiration. But there were, he supposed, a number of adequate reasons why Wally might have decided to grass. Maybe Johnson had screwed his girl. Or maybe Wally was just broke.

Or maybe ...

Clegg's hand flashed across and grasped Wally's bruised face between thumb and forefinger. Wally yelped and tore his face away.

'Did Johnson do that?'

'I told you, I did it on a doorhandle.'

'So that's it. Johnson belted you and you're getting your own back?'

Wally looked at the detective, and realized Clegg was pleased with this explanation.

'He wanted me to lend him money. He hit me 'cause I hadn't got any.'

Clegg gave him a hard look. 'If you've cooked this up to get your own back ... '

'Honest, Mr Clegg.'

Clegg sneered, but it was a reflex. Never let anybody see what you're thinking says the good book, and Clegg was thinking it sounded all right. A bit vague, which you'd expect from a junkie, and no more than a pointer. Would Wally know where to stop if he was trying to stitch up Toe-Rag?

'Do you know where he was hiding the stuff?'

'No, I had a look but I wasn't sure which alley it was. I cleared off when I saw some old bat clocking me. Look, if it's any good, that charge of possession you pulled me on the other week, will you drop it?'

'We'll see if it's any good first. I can't promise, anyway.'

'What about some money, then?'

'Money? For information that's got whiskers on it? You must be fucking joking. I ought to run you in for wasting my time. Johnson may not have been near the place for years.'

'Come on, Mr Clegg. It must be worth a tenner.'

'You're daydreaming, Wally. And if you've given me a lot of shit you'd best overdose. It'll be quicker and nicer than what I'll do to you. Now piss off.'

Clegg's news came as a welcome break to a murder squad in the doldrums. The shebeen inquiries had petered out. Detectives tramped the streets sixteen hours a day on ever-widening door-to-door inquiries. None of the Ridley detectives' informants had produced any useful information, and while Mick O'Hanlon passed on some fascinating stuff about the sexual predilections of some the town's more solid citizens, his sisters had not come up with the murderer of PC James.

Pryke was having lunch in the pub – bottle of Scotch and a knife and fork, said Nicholas – when Clegg burst in. Clegg forced his way past a crowd which included Hopkins, Fullalove and Gotobed. 'A quiet word please Guv'nor?' he asked.

Pryke's eyes glistened as he heard Clegg out. 'Drink up,' he told the others. 'We're going.'

At the station messengers were dispatched to round up the murder squad, and soon its members were pouring into the murder room, where Pryke, Hopkins and Clegg were clustered around the six-inch map.

'We'll search both sides of the road,' Pryke said. 'If he's still using the area it might not be the same alley. Send to Southampton for a pair of drug sniffers.' These were dogs trained to smell out drugs and used mainly to search ships for cannabis.

Pryke also asked the head of Ridley Division for a score of Uniform men, then called the squad to order. He briefed it on Clegg's tip without specifying where it came from, and went on to describe the alleys they would be searching.

'They're a bit unusual. They go alongside one house in four, make a right-angled turn left, past the rear gardens of three houses, directly into the garden of the fourth. We don't know what the hiding place might be. It need be no more than a bit of scraped-out cement to hide a few grains of heroin in, say, a twist of paper. It is literally a case of leaving no stone unturned. Check for loose bricks, large stones, slates, anything of that sort. Take your time and pay special attention to the gardens of empty houses. He's not likely to use the gardens of occupied houses.'

Ritchie listened to the briefing with rising excitement. So that bastard Johnson was back in the reckoning, was he. Ritchie, sucked into the door-to-door inquiries, had been unable to pursue his suspicions about Johnson and frustration had been growing within him as it had within everybody else. Now the squad seemed infused with a new sense of purpose. Pryke threw himself into the briefing as never before, and when he finished the room emptied fast. In a few seconds only Nicholas was left. Ritchie, one of the last out of the door, looked over his shoulder and was fleetingly surprised at the look of scepticism on the reader's face.

'No chance we're being set up, I suppose?' he asked Hopkins as they got into a car.

To his surprise, Hopkins also seemed unconvinced. 'Set up? Don't be silly. You heard Mr Pryke. Clegg's just brought the tablets from Mount Sinai. Let's wait and see what we find and how easily we find it.'

At first it seemed as though the information was useless, if not entirely erroneous. The men were divided into teams working both sides of the road from the ends into the middle, where the mobile incident room was converted into Pryke's headquarters. Pryke paced up and down like a general who, having committed his troops, can only wait in agony for the result.

The first reports were bad. As each alley was cleared Pryke's face grew longer and his response to questions more savage until at last he sat in his own car, staring straight ahead.

Conversely, as the cache grew more difficult to find, the sceptics were more prepared to believe in the good faith of Clegg's informant. If it had been a set-up surely the evidence would have been left where it could be found?

Eventually the search teams met up and the street was pronounced clean. Hopkins asked Pryke: 'What now?'

'Wait for the dogs,' said Pryke briefly, and wound up the window of his car. But Hopkins knew he no longer believed.

Even Ritchie felt a twinge of sympathy for Pryke. He did not know that Pryke's career was at risk, but the greenest policeman would understand Pryke's fear of failure in this case.

The inability of the CID to make headway was already responsible for tension between it and Uniform. In the queue for tea and buns the detectives found themselves the target for jokes that had a sharp edge of insult to them. A young detective constable, newly moved over from Uniform, was showing signs of losing his cool at the ragging of his former colleagues. Ritchie and a uniformed sergeant moved in to separate the men. The sergeant was Clay, the station officer on the night of the murder.

'Told you the Yard should've been called in,' Clay said. 'We've been pissing around for a couple of weeks now without getting anywhere. That prick Pryke couldn't catch a rubber duck in a bathtub.'

Ritchie shrugged. 'Only fairies have magic wands.'

'Must be enough in CID to start a bonfire, then,' said Clay. They watched a dog van labelled Hampshire Constabulary draw up.

'Maybe these will sniff something out,' said Ritchie, glad enough to change the subject.

The men watched the dogs work in and out of the alleys. Six or eight houses from the Mafeking Avenue end, Clegg had said. The houses went in fours, and when the first three alleys on each side had been cleared hope faded. Prematurely.

It was from the alley beside the sixteenth house on the evens side that an excited baying was heard. Pryke, who had been sitting motionless, head sunk on chest like Napoleon on the retreat from Moscow, turned reluctantly towards the sound, unwilling to hope but unable to prevent himself. One of the handlers emerged from the alley and beckoned the control point.

Nobody had ever seen Pryke move so fast. Out of the van in a single movement, he shot across to the alley. He turned the corner and saw the dogs springing at a six-foot wall.

'Bring a ladder,' he ordered.

He forced himself to appear calm and motioned Ritchie up when the ladder arrived.

Ritchie felt along the ridged coping stones until one shifted. He eased it off. In the frog of the brick underneath lay a twist of manila paper. He called for tweezers, lifted the paper carefully and bore it down.

'Back to the control van,' said Pryke briefly.

A space was cleared on a work surface. Using two pairs of tweezers the paper was straightened out. It was an envelope. Pryke turned it gently upside-down and a rough cube of vegetable matter fell out.

'Cannabis,' said Clegg.

Pryke shook the envelope. Two tiny pills rolled on to the table.

'And heroin,' said Clegg.

Kimberley Road again became the scene of intense police activity. Photographers took pictures of the alley, the wall and the brick where the envelope was found.

'What if it's a plant?' asked Hopkins. Pryke's face darkened.

Ritchie felt a shiver of premonition. He's beyond reason, he thought. He's bet too much emotional capital on this. But Pryke's training asserted itself.

'Check the surrounding houses. See if there's been any suspicious activity in the past few days. If it was planted it must have been done recently.'

He waited impatiently until the detectives returned with negative reports. The sun broke through his clouded face and he ordered everybody back to the station.

Pryke closeted himself with Hopkins and Clegg.

'Do we tell the Chief?' asked the latter.

'Can't wait to take the credit, can you?' Pryke sneered. 'Patience, Sergeant. I want to know more about your snout first.'

He got the name and other details and sent Clegg home along with the rest of the squad. Technicians were called in. They checked the envelope for fingerprints without success. The tablets and the vegetable matter were dispatched to the Home Office laboratories at Cardiff to make sure that they did not turn out to be compressed leaves and saccharine tablets. The photographers were given instructions which kept them at work until the small hours. Finally even Hopkins went home. Pryke went to the pub and drank alone until closing time.

It was nearly midnight when Wally answered an insistent knock on his door. As he turned the handle the door burst in on him and Pryke charged into the room, his face murderous. 'Right, you little shit,' he snarled, slamming Wally against the wall. 'What do you mean by planting that dope?'

The conversation that followed was a short one. The door to Wally's room opened and Pryke left without looking back at the youth who was still standing against the wall, staring as though mesmerized, white with shock.

From his home Pryke rang Whaley and told him of the find of heroin in Kimberley Road.

9

At next day's conference the reason why the photographers were working late was made plain.

'Door-to-door inquiries,' said Pryke to a subdued chorus of groans. He held up a thick loose binder. 'We've printed up pictures of all those known users of heroin we've got on our files. We want everybody living in or regularly passing through Mafeking Avenue and Kimberley Road to see if they can pick anybody out. There are twenty-four pictures in this album, all heavy users, many known to do a bit of pushing on the side. We haven't had time to print more but we think only an old hand or a pusher would use this sort of place of concealment.

'Obviously we want a positive ID on any of the people in the album, but our suspicions centre on Ralph Johnson, known to most of you as Toe-Rag Johnson, who has convictions for assault against the police and other acts of violence and has been known to carry a knife.' Pryke indicated the picture of Johnson, which was third in the album, and continued to remind the squad of the man's iniquities.

A worm of disquiet bored into Ritchie's brain. The Guv'nor's going it a bit, he thought uneasily. It was almost as though he was saying: 'This is our man. Let's get him.'

Pryke continued: 'Johnson was known to PC James. Let's suppose James stopped him while he was carrying drugs and a weapon. Johnson would know that with his record it would mean another heavy fall, so it might have made sense to kill him.'

As the briefing moved to its conclusion Ritchie was thoroughly disturbed. 'It's like a Judge Jeffries summing up,' he whispered to Nicholas, who was standing next to him. 'Consider the evidence carefully, then find the accused guilty.' Nicholas nodded. Ritchie looked round in vain for signs of similar disquiet on the faces of his colleagues, but saw only eagerness. At last they were zeroing in. He tried to extinguish his doubts. Emotional fervour had a counter-effect on him, he knew, and the harder a case was pleaded the less inclined he was, sometimes, to believe in it.

Pryke called for questions. Ritchie hesitated before saying: 'Surely Johnson's motive is not so strong as that. If he had punched James and run he could have ditched the heroin and the knife. If he was recognized he would only be charged with assaulting a police officer – six months at the most. Perhaps even a suspended sentence.'

Pryke did not welcome the comment. 'These are just pointers. I'm not suggesting we go to court on them. As for whether it was worth his while to kill James, only he can answer that, if he did it. He might have been hopped up at the time.'

'If he was high, what was he doing there at three o'clock in the morning?' said Dave Nicholas.

'He might have been shooting up when James tried to pinch him,' said Clegg.

'A mile from his home?' said Ritchie, disbelievingly. 'Is he likely to hide his stuff so far away that he has to cross half the town to get his fix?'

Pryke, showing the familiar signs of rage, snapped: 'I should wait until he's been arrested before you offer your services to the defence. Let's get it clear, witnesses are to be given a free hand to go through the album. We may think Johnson is the most likely, but we will not try to force our choice on anybody. Does that satisfy Sergeant Ritchie and Inspector Nicholas? Right, your albums are on the table at the side. Let's get down to it.'

Ritchie leafed through the pictures. Johnson's was third. Was it being unduly cynical to wonder if this position had been carefully calculated? Some people did not like to pick out the first of anything. Others would start to get bored towards the end of the book.

It was not that he no longer believed that Johnson was the killer. But he felt that the investigation had lost balance. If, by normal patient policework, they had tied it down to Johnson, nobody would have been more pleased than he. It was the miraculous 'breakthrough' he distrusted. 'Just too bloody convenient,' he confided to Nicholas, 'for Pryke, for Clegg and probably for whoever tipped Clegg off.'

As he reached the end of the book he sensed something missing. He turned back and went through them again but could not put his finger on it.

He looked up. Pryke, the only person left in the room, was watching him closely.

'Have you decided to join the investigation, Sergeant?' he inquired with menacing courtesy. 'Or would you prefer a return to general duties?'

'No fear, Guv,' Ritchie said stoutly. 'I want to see this case through.'

'Oh, I *am* glad,' said Pryke. 'Then I suggest you get out on the road.'

Hopkins divided the men into two squads, one under himself, one under Fullalove. Ritchie went in the latter, having already decided he would have no part of whatever game Pryke might be playing. No lingering suggestively over Johnson's picture, or 'accidentally' letting a witness know about his record of violence.

He drew a blank, a succession of shaken heads, although occasionally a finger would point at a face and the interviewee would say doubtfully: 'I think I've seen him before.' After that it was a matter of trying to tie him down to time, date and place. Did he see him recently? In this area? Acting furtively or normally?

And hearing answers like: 'I couldn't swear,' or: 'Not recently,' or: 'Doesn't he hang around that cafe in the Arcade?'

When Ritchie had cleared his first batch he went back to control. 'Any joy?' he asked Fullalove.

'Gotobed thinks he's got something, a sighting of Johnson. He's working on the witness now.'

If Ritchie had been asked to bet on who would come up with a sighting his money would have rested on the ambitious Gotobed.

Ritchie's only positive sighting during the entire day was one man who picked out Johnson. After a great deal of patient questioning he recalled that Johnson had once had a Christmas job in the store where he worked. Ritchie phoned the store, records were checked, and the man's recollections were confirmed. Another 'witness' written off.

By mid-afternoon every house in Kimberley Road and Mafeking Avenue had been visited at least once. The squad stood down until seven o'clock, when they would be back to catch people home from work.

Ritchie went home. He seemed hardly to have been there for weeks. Karen, who had just started a job as a temporary postwoman for the Christmas rush, greeted him with news of her day. Ritchie realized with a sense of shock that there were only a few days to Christmas and he had no presents yet. He sat at the dining room table sipping a large mug of tea.

'How's the job going, Dad?' asked Karen.

He grunted. 'It's a mess. For two weeks we've been scratching around like a dog with fleas, without a lead to bless ourselves with. Then suddenly a secret informant tells Clegg all about something which happened years ago and we grab it as though it was a gift from God, find what we're supposed to find, conclude that we're supposed to conclude and all of a sudden Pryke is Sherlock Holmes, Maigret and Superintendent Barlow all rolled into one. Somebody'll end up combing shit from his hair before we're through.'

Janet had come in. 'Make sure it isn't you. Keep your head down. It's not your responsibility.'

Her advice was distilled from generations of police lore. It's the Governor's job to take the responsibility so stay mum and keep your lip buttoned. Nobody likes a pushy subordinate, especially if he's right. Ritchie shuddered with annoyance.

'Pryke's already rumbled that I'm less than enthusiastic over this new "break". He thinks he's got Toe-Rag Johnson all tied up with ribbon. Buggered if I do.'

Janet regarded him acidly: 'For God's sake, what's the matter with you? When you put Johnson down last time you said he should have got life. So why stick your neck out for him now?' She was bewildered. It simply did not make sense.

Karen was shocked. 'What are you saying, Mum? That it doesn't matter whether he goes down for something he might not have done? I thought Dad was supposed to be in the justice industry?'

'Justice!' Janet said witheringly. 'It isn't his job to decide what's just. He's to put up the villains for the court to decide.'

This, too, was conventional police wisdom. But by the mere act of accusing somebody, the police were putting him in peril. 'You're both missing the point,' said Ritchie, rising. 'Johnson's done enough to be put behind bars for life, in my book. But if he gets done for this murder, and didn't do it, then whoever did has got away with it.'

'It's appearances that count,' said Janet. 'A policeman killed, a man convicted. That's what the public want.'

'Did you know your mother had the makings of a Nazi?' said Ritchie to Karen, on his way out to do his Christmas shopping.

He struggled through his shopping, paying more than he needed because he did not have time to hunt down apposite bargains. Janet, Karen, Mum, Ma and Pa-in-law and Eileen, he ticked off the names. That's all, except for cards.

Ritchie liked funny, sexy cards and decided to visit a specialist shop. Dodging through the Christmas crowds he weaved down the Arcade, eyes searching faces, a habit ingrained by years of self-training.

His attention was commanded by a tall ungainly figure diving into a branch arcade. Wally Stolz doing his Christmas shopping, he thought. A dozen disposable syringes, gift-wrapped.

He stopped suddenly, barely noticing cursing shoppers colliding with him. That was it. Wally Stolz. German-born son of a former prisoner-of-war who had returned to live in this country in 1950. Heavy user of heroin, convictions for possession and theft. An occasional pusher.

'Why wasn't Stolz's picture in that album?' he asked aloud.

'Why wasn't Stolz's picture in that album?'

Clegg snapped his fingers: 'Stolz! Of course. I ought to have included him. I forgot. He's supposed to have come off H. He's attending a drug addiction clinic.' His face was guileless. Ritchie did not believe a word.

'Come off it. That lasted about three weeks, for Christ's sake. He's on bail for possession now. You nicked him.'

'Well, he slipped my mind.'

'Is he your snout?'

Clegg bristled: 'You know better than to ask. I don't say who my snouts are, any more than you do.'

Ritchie ignored him. ' ... Because if he is, this information's not worth a pinch of shit. He's got a hundred reasons for wanting to stitch up Toe-Rag, not least that Toe-Rag once stitched him up, or so he claims.'

'Get off my back, Ritchie,' said Clegg. 'What's the matter, don't you like it when somebody else's snouts come up with the goods?'

'Fuck you, Jimmy,' said Ritchie with contempt. 'I've got enough sense to know when to look a snout's information up, over and under before getting forty coppers to work on it.'

'Why don't you tell Pryke he's been conned, then?' sneered Clegg, and walked away.

'Why wasn't Stolz's picture in that album?' Ritchie asked Pryke at the briefing for the evening's inquiries.

Pryke, who had been warned by Clegg, did not bat an eyelid. 'Our inquiries have already ruled him out.'

'Beg your pardon, Guv'nor, but if this information came from Stolz I reckon we ought to be careful because ... '

Pryke blew up. He strode down to Ritchie. 'What the hell do you think you're doing discussing informants in public? I've told you Stolz has been ruled out, and that should be good enough for you. Do you think I'm going to consult a bloody sergeant over every detail of this case? By God I've had enough of you, Ritchie. Everybody's pulling on the same line but you. If you can't work as part of a team, we'll find you some dustbin jobs to do. You're off this detail. Any more of this and you'll be returned to general duties.'

Ritchie was shaken. 'With all due respect, Guv'nor ... ' he started. Pryke turned his back and returned to the front. 'With all due respect,' he mimicked. 'With all due respect ... '

'With all due respect, Sergeant Ritchie, you're too bloody big for your boots. With all due respect, due respect is what you're lacking. You can't pass your bloody exams but you try to tell me how to run the squad.'

There was a silence. Some of the squad detectives moved away from Ritchie as though he had the plague. The briefing for the evening's door-to-door inquiries was completed. At the end Pryke told Hopkins to find some work for Ritchie.

Hopkins was cool and matter-of-fact, for which Ritchie was grateful. He checked through the 'things to be done' book. 'You haven't seen Hagley yet. Might as well do that. It'll be another loose end out of the way.'

'A dustbin job,' thought Ritchie viciously, as he rang the doorbell at Hagley's house.

Hagley was fresh-faced and short-haired. He wore an expression in which amiability and naïvety were commingled. He was eager to help.

'Have you found who did it?'

'It's a slog. We are hoping you can help us.' It was one of those innocent phrases which just might seem loaded with accusation to guilty ears. Not this time.

'If I can, but I don't see how. It's the most dreadful thing, isn't it? I've never really known anybody who has died, let alone been murdered.'

Lucky you, thought Ritchie, who had known too many, and prepared to take a statement.

It was the same dreary recital of virtue. When it came to an end Ritchie asked about James's interest in music.

'Music? I don't think so particularly.'

'No? I met Muck ... Mr Sendle. He said Rodney was interested in music.'

'Oh, he did go through a thing after Sendle came. He started a music club. There were only a few boys in it. I joined with Rodney and we used to go to London or Bristol or Bath for concerts, but it declined. I think there were only one or two trips last year. Rodney lost interest after a year or so, and stopped going.'

'Any particular reason?'

'I don't think so. Perhaps Mr Sendle's taste was a little too astringent. He liked Mahler and Shostakovich and chamber music. Rodney's taste ran more to romantic music like *Swan Lake* or operetta.'

Ritchie ruminated. Sendle had not mentioned these musical outings. 'How many boys went to these concerts?'

'At first anything up to a dozen, but it dropped. They were called off when the numbers dropped to four.'

'So never less than four went?'

'Unless somebody went sick at the last moment.'

Hagley hesitated. 'There was one time when Sendle and Rodney went to a concert alone. There had been one of those sudden flu bugs. People who were right as rain in the morning were developing temperatures by the afternoon. But it was something Rodney particularly wanted to hear, so they went. I think it was the last time Rodney went to a concert.'

'Why? Did they have a row?'

'No, I don't think so. Rodney was already going less often by that time.'

Ritchie hesitated over the next step, afraid of what he might do to Sendle, knowing that a mere suggestion that he was suspected by the police might put the man's job in jeopardy. But he felt he had no choice.

'Did Sendle have any reputation for being bent? You know, queer?'

Hagley looked shocked. 'Oh no. Well, we knew he was a bachelor, of course, and there were always people who made smutty jokes and insinuations, but never any serious suggestions.'

'Did he like boys, make friends with them? Did he ever try to be alone with boys – you, for instance?'

'No. And not with Rodney either. I don't remember ever being alone with Sendle for more than a few minutes.'

'What about Rodney? Was he queer?'

Hagley flushed angrily: 'Look here, I want to help you but this isn't fair. Rodney's dead and can't answer you and you're trying to blacken his name. You'll be suggesting I'm queer in a minute.'

'Are you?'

'No!'

Ritchie allowed a silence to fall. After a few moments he said: 'Rodney's a hero at the moment, and the whole police force would rather he remained one. We think he was probably killed by a criminal trying to avoid arrest, but we've got to clear away other possibilities and that means asking questions about his sex life among other things. It may not be pleasant, but it has to be done. Do you understand?'

'Yes,' muttered Hagley, hating Ritchie.

'You were his best friend?'

'I suppose so. I used to be, but I hadn't seen him in weeks.'

'But you used to go to the cinema regularly?'

'Not since we left school. Oh, once I think, a week or so after he joined the force. Not since then. I used to ring him regularly to suggest films we might see, but he always made some excuse, so in the end I got fed up and told him to phone me when he felt like seeing something.'

Ritchie said: 'But his father said he went out with you regularly.'

'Not for months.'

Well, well, thought Ritchie. So PC James did have his secrets after all. He took a further statement, in which he included the name of the last film they had seen together, to establish dates — Hagley remembered only that it was on a Tuesday — then went on to Hagley's brush with Toe-Rag Johnson.

Hagley shrugged. 'He hit me and took my dinner money and some pocket money off me, and got expelled. I saw him in town occasionally but I always tried to avoid him in case he hit me again for getting him into trouble. I never knew Rodney had any interest in Johnson, but I suppose knowing him personally and as a criminal he might have done once he became a policeman.'

Ritchie added that to the statement and left with food for thought. Hagley had fleshed James out a bit, made him less of a one-dimensional figure and added a bit of mystery. The likelihood was that it meant nothing. Though James might have been a homosexual, there could be other reasons for his secretiveness. He might have embarked on an affair with a woman his family would have disapproved of, somebody much older than himself, or with a reputation for immorality. Anything like that made a crime passionnel a possibility.

But highly bloody unlikely at between two and three in the morning, out in the street.

Better see James senior again. And Sendle. Poor old Mucky. Check if he's got any form.

10

MRS JAMES came to the door. She did not recognize Ritchie, who reintroduced himself. He was led to where James senior was seated, staring at the picture of his son on the fireplace.

Ritchie gave as his pretext for coming the fact that he had not yet spoken to Mrs James. He listened patiently while she told what he labelled 'the orthodox version'. When she came to the end he said: 'Both you and your husband have said Rodney went to the pictures with Desmond Hagley. When would be the last time that happened?'

James answered: 'About two days, maybe three, before he died. Why?'

'I've spoken to Hagley and he says the last time he went out with Rodney was months ago. Did Rodney tell you specifically he was going out with Desmond? Or did you just assume it because that's who he usually went out with?'

'Well, both I suppose. I mean, I'm sure he has told us within the past few weeks that he was going out with Desmond.'

Mrs James said: 'I've asked several times because I wanted to know if he was making friends in the police force. He always said it was Desmond. Why should he lie?'

'Why should Desmond lie?' asked Ritchie. 'Let's go back to girlfriends. Would he have thought you would be against him having a regular girl?'

'We would have been pleased,' said the woman. 'We always hoped he would find himself a nice girl.'

'Supposing he was having sex with one? Would you still be pleased?'

Mrs James answered obliquely. 'Morals are changing, aren't they? I don't think I would expect his standards to be any different to other people's.'

'Would he know that?'

'We've always discussed morality openly.'

'There are all sorts of other possibilities. An affair with an older woman. That's quite likely for a young lad, shy with girls of his own age. Or with somebody he might know you would disapprove of.'

'I didn't know of any such thing. I suppose if he wasn't with Desmond he must have had some secret.'

James said heavily: 'Go and make some tea, Ma.'

When she had gone he stood up. 'For God's sake, what are you doing? She thinks of him as a hero. If he was killed by a criminal is it fair that she should have to go through this? Learning that her boy had a guilty secret?'

'How do you know it was a guilty secret?'

He sighed. 'Because I had to put a stop to something once. While he was at school. He had what you might call a crush on somebody. I saw the other person and put a stop to it.'

'Who was it?'

'I'm not going to say. It can't possibly be relevant to this.'

'You'll have to leave that to us to judge. Was it a homosexual affair?'

'It wasn't an affair, for God's sake. It was calf love.'

'Was it Alwyn Sendle?'

James froze. He looked at Ritchie with a kind of bitter respect. 'You've really worked hard at digging up dirt, haven't you? Yes, it was Sendle.

'It was Marilyn who warned me. She said Rodney and Sendle seemed to be very close, especially since they had been to a concert together. I made inquiries about Sendle and when I found he was unmarried it was enough for me. I went to see him and told him I didn't want a close association between him and Rodney. Both of them told me that there was nothing more than a joint interest in music, and personal friendship, so I left it at that.'

'How long ago did this happen?'

'About two years ago.'

'Did you report it to the headmaster?'

'No. I didn't want to ruin Sendle. And Rodney begged me not to take it any further. I felt quite sorry for the man. I think it was just a case of he had certain tendencies. I'm not saying he gave way to them. I just thought it an unhealthy relationship.'

'Did they stop seeing each other?'

'I'm sure they did. I kept my eye on Rodney for a long time after that and his time always seemed accounted for.'

Mrs James carried a tea tray in from the kitchen. There was an uncomfortable silence until James had a further inspiration. He rummaged in his pockets. 'I've run out of cigarettes, love. Would you mind popping out to the corner shop?' Mrs James looked bewildered, but she went. Something stirred in Ritchie's memory.

'Last time I came you told me you phoned Rodney the night he was murdered, and asked him to bring some cigarettes home. Right?'

'Yes. I can't face the day without one.'

'When you called him back you had an argument. What was it about?'

'An argument? We didn't have an argument.'

'The station officer overheard it. He said Rodney seemed to be trying to calm you down.'

James looked bewildered. 'He must be mistaken. I didn't call him back. Whoever he was speaking to, it wasn't me.'

Ritchie took another statement from James covering the relationship of his son with Sendle and dropped it on Nicholas's desk along with Hagley's. In the 'Things to be Done' book he entered a note to get a statement from Sgt Clay, the station officer who had mentioned the telephone call, cross-referenced everything and went home.

Janet was waiting for him in a mood of barely repressed venom. The wife network had been in operation and she had heard about the row with Pryke.

'You bloody fool,' she stormed without preamble. 'I told you not to shoot your mouth off. The way you're going you'll end up directing traffic. Christ, why did I have to marry such a bonehead?'

'Just struck lucky, I guess,' said Ritchie, burying himself in the evening paper.

Janet bored on, her voice shrill: 'You realize you're the laughing stock of the family?'

'Your family, not mine. I'm a copper, a sergeant, I've got my own house and a daughter in college. They think I'm marvellous.'

'You'll be a marvel, all right, if you survive this one.'

Ritchie let her go on, his face setting stonily. 'All right,' he said at last. 'You've had your say. If you've got any sense, you'll drop it.'

The remark only served to build up the pressure of her wrath. She tripped over her tongue in her determination to subject his shortcomings to a comprehensive review.

When she paused for breath Ritchie said mildly: 'I suppose you realize you suffer from the same fault? Not knowing when to shut up?'

'In my case it doesn't matter.'

'That does put me in my place,' he said. 'Don't bother to wait up.' He stalked out of the house and, feeling quite pleased with himself, drove round to Eileen's house.

'Hello, stranger, I thought you'd gone off me,' she said.

'Never. I've just been tucked up.'

'The murder, I suppose. And I'd really been looking forward to that week. Goes to show, never anticipate anything with a copper. Something always goes wrong.'

He gave her his Christmas present, the gift wrapping slightly grubby and smelling of rubber because he had hidden it behind the spare wheel of his car. She dug the perfume out and gave him a thank you kiss. She looked amused and suddenly he remembered he had given her the same thing last year.

She gave him a book and he turned it over dubiously. He never read much except newspapers and official papers. 'You'll like it,' she said. 'It's sexy. Do you want to go to bed?'

'Mmmm. It's an idea.'

She whisked into the bathroom and he undressed, listening to the sloshing of water. He was in bed by the time she came back, dusted with talcum and dowsed with the scent he had given her.

She bounced happily on the bed before hauling his fourteen stone on top of her. 'We must be like hippos mating,' she said with a giggle. 'All hip and bottomus.'

Afterwards she asked drowsily how the case was going. Ritchie told her. Eileen sat up. 'That's awful,' she said. 'Can he do that? Just because you asked some questions?'

'He can put me back into uniform without a by-your-leave if he wants. He may do it too. Pryke likes people to agree with him.'

'How does a man like that get to be where he is?'

'Sod's law, which says of several possible courses of action the worst will be the one that's chosen. Then all you can say is: "Sod it." It's specially relevant in the police force.'

'You don't mean you're going to let this man Johnson be fitted up — is that the right word? — and do nothing about it? And stop that.' She swatted his hand away.

Exasperated, Ritchie said: 'There's nothing I can do. Pryke told me to keep my nose out. He says Stolz has been eliminated from the inquiry, and he's the boss.'

'Couldn't you show Stolz's picture around Kimberley Road and see if anybody recognizes him?'

'And get shot for it? It's like the army, don't you understand? The commanding officer may be drunk, reading his maps upside-down and be pointing the wrong way, but if he says charge, you have to charge.'

'Well, to me it sounds like cowardice.'

'Isn't that bloody lovely. One woman in my life tells me to shut up and do as I'm told, and you and Karen want me to risk my pension for Toe-Rag Johnson.'

'Janet,' said Eileen, 'is a cow. You should have married me.'

'You weren't around when you were needed.'

Eileen snuggled up to him. 'It's the fact you could retire in a few years that's holding you back isn't it? A pension makes cowards of us all.'

Ritchie laughed, but he found the comment rankling as Eileen dropped off to sleep. It was absurd to think of sticking his neck out for scum like Johnson. Janet would be unbearable if she knew he was even contemplating it.

The thought popped into his mind that, if it proved to be the final straw between him and Janet, it might be worth it. With Karen almost finished college, what was there to keep them together? But if it cost him his job in CID? He'd resign rather than go back into uniform.

No, he decided. It was ridiculous. But Eileen's jibe still hurt.

In the murder room Pryke and Hopkins gloomily considered the meagre results of the day's effort. Out of hundreds of interviews by forty policemen there were only five alleged sightings of Johnson, one from an elderly couple conned out of £50 by cowboy builders one of whom, they thought, resembled Johnson.

Hopkins shook his head. 'We know about this team. One does look a bit like Johnson. It isn't though.'

Another sighting was better. A woman who had been at Thomas Hardy School with Johnson had seen him in the area. 'About three months ago. He wasn't doing anything in particular or acting oddly. Just walking down the road.'

'She might be useful but she's nowhere near enough. What about Gotobed's two? They're supposed to have seen Johnson acting suspiciously. How reliable would you say Gotobed is, Hoppy?'

'Makes up in enthusiasm what he lacks in experience,' Hopkins said tactfully. He added: 'He probably hypnotized them to get the answers he wanted.'

Pryke re-read the statements. 'Vague,' he said. 'Somebody answering the description of Johnson seen acting furtively. Not sure when, must have been several weeks ago. We've got to harden this up or we've got sweet F-A to take to court.'

'Stolz?'

'Do me a favour. Says Johnson hid his drugs there three, maybe four years ago. That concludes the case for the prosecution, M'Lud.'

'OK. What do we do?'

'Work on all of them until they'd identify Johnson as their mothers if necessary. Then put Johnson up for an identity parade.'

'If they don't pick him out we've had it unless Johnson coughs.'

'That's right,' said Pryke heavily. 'Johnson's got to cough. If we can make him admit he once used this area to hide his stuff we're in with a chance.'

11

At that moment the object of these discussions was returning to Ridley on the Bristol train. He had been on his feet for most of the day and his face was grey with grime and fatigue. But his eyes were bright. He felt alert and able to deal with anything.

The previous day his girlfriend, Alison Parker, had received her Christmas bonus and handed him fifteen pounds. He had left for London immediately, travelling in the rush hour because there would be no ticket inspection and he had not wanted to waste money by paying his fare. He jumped the train when it halted at signals outside Paddington Station and made his way across London, skipping on to buses, and off again as soon as he was asked for his fare. When he reached Forest Gate he bought five prescriptions for heroin at three pounds apiece from a crooked doctor. He had two made out for that day and the other three post-dated at three-day intervals.

He went to the West End and obtained heroin for the two scripts dated that day and shot up in the men's lavatories at Piccadilly underground station.

With his heroin and scripts in his pocket he had no further use for the capital. He caught a Ridley train by picking up a discarded ticket and running past the inspector seconds before the guard signalled it away.

He left his coat containing the drugs and remaining scripts on a luggage rack above the head of a coatless traveller, sat for a few moments then moved up the train. He found an engaged lavatory, rapped sharply and said: 'Tickets, please.' A woman said: 'Hold on, I'm coming,' and Johnson moved on quickly.

At the next door a ticket was pushed out, but it was a half fare.

He tried two more doors before getting the return half of a day fare from Ridley to London. With such a ticket he could travel like a gentleman instead of dodging the inspector for ninety minutes. He found a day-old newspaper and a seat in another compartment and settled down, leaving his coat where it was in case some evil copper had spotted him boarding the train and had wired ahead for him to be intercepted and searched at an intermediate station.

He waited until the train was approaching Ridley before he recovered his coat and took up station beside the end door of a coach. The train passed a hamlet, ran through fields and into a tunnel. Johnson let the window down in the roaring darkness and started counting the telegraph poles after the train emerged into the light and began to lose speed for the approach to Ridley station. When he reached the ninth pole he waited for a count of three before hurling the packet, which was weighted with a pebble, and watched with satisfaction as it cleared the fence and landed about fifteen feet east of the tenth pole.

With a valid ticket he could have enjoyed the luxury of going through the barrier at Ridley like an ordinary mortal. Prudence prevailed. Even out of date the ticket would have its uses and the station, built in a more trusting era, was as full of holes as a cheese. He waited until the press of disembarking passengers blocked the ticket inspector's view, then strolled down the platform onto the track. A signalman shouted but Johnson ignored him, knowing he could not leave his box, and crossed the goods terminal and into the street.

Half an hour and an unpaid-for bus journey later he had recovered his packet and was walking back into town. This was the most dangerous time. Despite the cold he walked with his hands outside his pockets, lightly balled. If he was jumped by the police he would hurl the packet away and try to recover it later. Johnson had been a target for the law for seven years and he had invented a number of techniques for evading search and arrest. The ritual was part of the thrill.

He had had a good day. But Johnson had to admit that the good days were rare now. There had been times when drugs had provided him with excitement and a good living; when he had terrorized the opposition and had come out on top by cunning or force. He had been, was still, tough. He kept in shape with weight training and had once been a promising boxer. Other users he held in contempt. Their drugs were a prop they needed because they could not face the truth about themselves.

Johnson told himself that he was different. To him heroin was an expression of his defiance of the straight world. He said it, and believed it, except that sometimes, as he was coming down from one fix and before he shot up again, he saw himself without illusion and shuddered at what he saw.

The days before his last sentence seemed like a golden age, so full of incident and excitement and victory had they been. In fact they had lasted about a year, including the four months he had drawn for the heroin powder in his jacket.

But when he had emerged from prison after the second sentence, everything was different. There were as many users as before, but they were less tightly knit. They avoided him and he could not escape the feeling they regarded him with contempt, like a survival from another era.

He was down and nearly out, living in a succession of sordid rooms whose landlords evicted late payers without bothering with the formalities of court orders. He existed on social security and Alison's wages, eating whatever she could filch from the department store where she worked.

Johnson relied on Alison more than he cared to admit. Once he had tried to prove his ruthlessness by bringing a man home who would pay to have sex with her. She humiliated him by walking out and he had to beg her to return.

Alison betrayed no disgust as he shot up, nor did she try to persuade him to come off drugs. 'You'll do it when you're ready,' she had said.

Wryly he admitted that her method might be more efficacious

than those of the highly qualified prison medical staff who for twenty-eight months, at a cost that would have equipped a small hospital ward, had tried to make his compulsory cure permanent. His answer, when he was released, had been to take the first train to London and use his release money to score in Soho.

Now he was beginning to want to kick his habit. It could even be interpreted as another victory against the straight world, that he could succeed on his own where its punishments and blandishments had totally failed.

The operation to pull Johnson in was to be a showpiece affair. Pryke wanted word to get around that a suspect had been arrested 'in connection with' the murder of PC James, knowing how the phrase would be interpreted.

Clegg was called in.

'Who's Johnson's landlord? Have we got anything on him?' demanded Pryke.

'He sells illegal alcohol. He's a Pole. Makes wood spirit.'

'That'll do.'

Clegg gave such details as he knew of Johnson's living habits. They decided to raid immediately in the hope of catching Johnson in bed and, with luck, some drugs in the flat. If not, they could be planted if they needed a holding charge.

Hopkins and Clegg called on the landlord.

'You been selling alcohol lately, Johnny?' inquired Hopkins.

'Stopped long time ago.'

'We've got information that says otherwise. Mind if we take a look round? Or if you do, here's a search warrant.'

The Pole shrugged: 'OK, you no find nothing. Where you want me to take you?'

'Nowhere. You give us the keys of your flats and we'll take a look. You just go off to the police station in that car.'

The Pole looked alarmed. 'You no plant nothing?'

'I'll pretend I didn't hear that,' said Hopkins. 'Do what you're told and don't push your luck.'

The Pole handed over several tagged bunches of keys and got into the car unhappily. 'Can I call my solicitor?'

'What for? If you've got no illegal alcohol you don't need him. If you have there's plenty of time. Stop beng a nuisance.'

The Pole was driven away and Hopkins radioed the squad who were to make the raid and positioned them conspicuously. They were armed. 'Make sure some of the guns are seen,' he told Fullalove.

Hopkins, Fullalove and Clegg let themselves into the house where Johnson lived with the glee of schoolboys on a scrumping expedition. They drew their guns and Hopkins and Clegg flattened themselves against the wall on either side of Johnson's door. 'I've always wanted to do this,' whispered Hopkins. Fullalove grinned. He leaned against the wall opposite the door and booted it near the handle with the sole of his shoe, using the wall as a launch pad for extra impetus. Hopkins and Clegg jumped for the opening and reeled back as their heads clashed. Fullalove hurled himself between them into the room and leaped into the approved police marksman stance, legs open, slightly crouched, holding the pistol two-handed at arm's length.

'You cunt,' he told Clegg, who had staggered in after him. 'It's the wrong room.' A black man and woman were sitting up in a bed made up on the floor. The blankets had slipped down to reveal her breasts, but she seemed oblivious of it. In a cot a baby was crying.

Hopkins proved equal to the occasion. 'Sorry you've been troubled,' he said. 'The landlord will mend the lock.' He ushered the others out and fixed Clegg with a look of burning contempt. 'Put those shooters away,' he told the rest of the squad as they left the house.

A white Mini hurtled round the corner and drew up, tyres screaming. Tompkins and a photographer tumbled out, feet entangled in safety belts in their haste. 'Hello, Hoppy,' said Tompkins. 'What's this about an armed raid?'

'Has somebody done a bank, then?' asked Hopkins blandly.

'A police raid. We heard you were round here, mob-handed with guns.'

'Somebody having you on. Can you see any guns?'

Tompkins had to admit he could not. 'What is happening, then?'

'You can't ask questions like that. What would Mr Pryke say? Still, as I know you. It's more door-to-door inquiries.'

The door of the raided house opened and the man they had surprised in bed peered out. He saw Hopkins and started to shut the door. Hopkins reached it in two strides. 'Just the chap. Could I have a word?' He pushed inside and shut the door firmly behind him.

'There you are,' said Fullalove. 'Nothing here for you. Best push along now.'

Tompkins hesitated, then returned to the car, not satisfied, but not sure what to do about it. They drove to the end of the street and stopped, watching the squad and watched by them. Eventually they drove off. The police piled back into their vehicles and returned to the station, leaving one man on the door with orders to prevent Tompkins gaining access to the house should he return.

Pryke rolled his eyes. 'I'm surprised at my restraint,' he said, sounding surprised. 'I must be getting used to cock-ups.'

'He lived there a couple of days ago,' said Clegg, helplessly. 'Ask the Polack.'

The landlord was brought in. 'OK?' he said. 'No alcohol?'

'Dunno yet,' said Hopkins. 'Where's Johnson and his bird gone?'

'Johnson? I thought you looking for alcohol.'

'Don't think. Just answer the question.'

'I throw him out yesterday. He owe three weeks rent.'

'Where's he gone?'

'I not know. He don't tell me and I don't ask.'

'OK, you can go. Incidentally, there's a room with a busted

lock at one of your houses. Tenants are entitled to a lock on their door so you'd better fix it.'

'Broken lock? All the locks all right this morning.'

'Well, it's not all right now. OK, bugger off.'

As the door closed behind the Pole Pryke told Clegg: 'Go and find out where Johnson lives. And do your best not to send us round to the convent unless you're certain he's shacked up with the Mother Superior.'

Tompkins returned to the house twice and found the policeman on the door. He left it until after dark and tried again. The watch had been withdrawn.

He was let in and directed to the room with a smashed lock, where he was told an extraordinary tale. Despite a police denial, the story was in next morning's papers, naming Johnson as the target of the raid.

Clegg, who had been circulating the town until the small hours, was in early explaining that Johnson seemed to have gone to ground. Miserably aware that his stock, which yesterday had seemed so high, was plummeting, he was still talking when a dapper and jaunty Johnson walked into Ridley police station waving a *Daily Mirror*. 'What's this shit about you looking for me with guns?' he demanded.

Johnson was taken to the CID floor and left in a waiting room. His appearance caused consternation. A voluntary surrender had not been part of the plan.

Pryke sat back, his chair leaning against the wall, eyes closed. 'Let the fucker go,' he said wearily.

Hopkins was astounded.

'Let him go,' repeated Pryke. 'He's no use like this. We'll nick him later in accordance with our original plan, except no guns this time.'

'What'll I tell him?'

'How should I know?'

'Get rid of him,' Hopkins told Clegg.

'What'll I tell him?'

'How should I know? But get his address.'

Clegg told Johnson. 'Nobody wants you. You must have made a mistake. Still, give me your address, just in case.'

Johnson unfolded the *Mirror* and showed the headline: 'Armed Police in "Wrong House" Raid'.

'What about this, then?'

'I should sue them,' said Clegg. 'You know your way out?'

Whaley shook his head over the papers in disbelief. 'I don't think I've ever known anything like it. I don't think I've ever known anything like this job from start to finish. And we haven't even finished yet. Is there any sort of reasonable explanation, Mr Pryke?'

'We had an anonymous tip-off that the man who killed PC James was holed up in that flat, armed with a sawn-off shotgun. In view of this Chief Inspector Hopkins filed a request for arms which went through the proper channels.'

'There's documentation to cover this, I suppose?'

'Message recorded in the book, arms properly indented for,' said Pryke. There was fatalism in his attitude. The time for excuses, whether valid or otherwise, was over. Only success mattered now.

Whaley sighed. 'I suppose it will all come out in the inquiry. Thank you, Mr Pryke.'

Pryke told Hopkins: 'We'll nick him again on Christmas Eve. And if there are any more cock-ups, Uniform Branch will get their biggest crop of recruits ever.'

Ritchie heard of the Johnson raid from an appalled Dave Nicholas. 'It's serious,' Nicholas protested as Ritchie roared with laughter.

How serious could be seen when Ritchie went to the canteen. Normally CID and Uniform mingled. Now they separated into two groups. No, three, for there was also a split in the CID ranks between Pryke's Praetorian Guard and those to whom the whole case reeked and who were determined to keep their heads down. As Ritchie and Nicholas weaved their way to a table they ran a gauntlet of hostile comment from both Uniform and the Pryke loyalists. They found an empty table and sat together.

'What about the queer angle?' Ritchie wanted to know. 'Does Pryke go for it?'

Nicholas shrugged. 'He said you could chase it. It would keep you out of his hair. Doesn't go a bundle on it. It's a bit vague isn't it? You know, something that might have happened a couple of years back?'

'Like the drug drop, you mean?'

'Like the drug drop. Well, Pryke's doing his thing. You might as well do yours. Statistically, more than sixty per cent of murders have a domestic origin so it doesn't make a lot of sense Pryke using all our effort on a forty per cent chance.'

Ritchie had spent the early part of the morning getting Sendle's address from the County Council because the schools had broken up for Christmas. After his coffee break he found the house, the central one of a short terrace in the old quarter of Ridley. It looked well cared for. There were no net curtains, and peering in Ritchie saw a grand piano, comfortable chairs and bookshelves covering a wall. There was no answer to his ring.

He tried the neighbours. On one side a bored housewife said she knew nothing about Sendle's habits, nor where he had gone nor when he would come home. She disappeared without displaying any curiosity about Ritchie's identity.

On the other side he had only to say he was a police officer to open the floodgates. A garrulous redhead said: 'Ooh! Is it boys? Frank always said we'd have the police round some day.'

'What do you mean?'

'Well, he's a bit of a queer, in't 'e? There's always these boys going in there.'

'Alone?'

'No,' she admitted reluctantly. 'In groups as far as I ever see.'

'What do they go there for, music?'

'There is music, usually.'

'Where do you get this business about him being queer from, then?'

'It's Frank, really. Hold on, I'll call him.'

Frank came to the door, shivering in trousers, vest and cardigan. He was short, fat and greasy and wore a confidential smile. 'Well, you know. Middle-aged bachelor and that, and them boys coming round. Stands to reason.'

'Never any girls?'

'Sometimes. Camouflage, innit?'

Ritchie showed a picture of Rodney James in school uniform which he had got from the photographer who had the contract with Thomas Hardy School. 'Ever seen him?'

'May've. Can't say as I ever looked that closely.'

His wife peered at the picture. ' 'e looks familiar,' she said, but Ritchie was almost sure it was wishful thinking. 'Who is 'e?'

'A boy missing from home. He's keen on music so we wondered if Mr Sendle knew him. Any idea where Mr Sendle might be?'

'School 'olidays, innit? He often goes away for a few days during the 'olidays. His parents live in Brum. He usually goes there.'

'Ta,' said Ritchie. 'Oh, and don't go spreading gossip, will you? Or he'll have you for slander. On what you've said to me he could have the shirts off your backs.' He sauntered off, leaving the shaken couple staring after him.

He took a turn round the back of the houses. They had long gardens and high walls pierced by doors. Standing on tiptoe he could just peer over them. Calculating which must be Sendle's, he assessed it as a clandestine access route. It was overlooked to some extent by frosted windows in neighbouring houses, probably bathrooms and lavatories. It would be safe enough at night.

He called back to the school photographer and asked to see his recent group pictures. He picked out Sendle and obtained an enlargement.

Ridley had two gay pubs. He showed his pictures round each, Sendle first. At the better class of the two he was greeted effusively by the barman, who recognized Sendle immediately. 'Oh, Alwyn, yes,' he drawled. 'He comes in quite often, although come to think of it I haven't seen him for a week or two.'

'How long has he been coming here?'

'Over a year, on and off.'

'With anybody?'

'For a time, yes. When he first came in he was a bit like a nun in a knocking shop, you know? He'd sit down with his vodka and orange all by himself, but if anybody suggested, you know, getting it together he'd shy away. We put him down as one of those poor people who just haven't, you know, come to terms with themselves. But a few months ago he started coming with ever such a nice young lad and we were so pleased because he's really rather a dear, you know, Alwyn I mean. Now what was the boy's name? Oh, Rodney, that's right. Yes, that picture does look like him, although of course he never came here with school uniform on, we wouldn't allow that. Asking for trouble, wouldn't it be?

'Anyway, Alwyn and Rodney must have had a bit of a tiff because they stopped coming for a bit and next time it was just Alwyn, alone again. It was ever so sad, you know.'

On his return to the police station Ritchie phoned the Criminal Records Office at the Yard. Half an hour later he got his answer. Sendle had a conviction, three years before, in Bradford. For gross indecency. A call to Bradford police furnished him with the sad, sordid, commonplace details. A public lavatory notorious as a homosexual haunt had been kept under observation for a day. Sendle was one of thirty men arrested. His trade had been given as unemployed clerk.

Ritchie stared at his notes and wished he had found some other way of earning a living. Sendle's sad face swam into his mind. A public lavatory for God's sake! In his uniformed days he too had arrested homosexuals in public lavatories. It was always considered to be something of a joke, and he had never allowed the ashen faces of professional men staring ruin in the face to interfere with the hilarious recounting of the day's events in the canteen afterwards. Why did they do it? Surely they must realize that arrest was sooner or later inevitable? Perhaps that was what they wanted. That would be a psychiatrist's explanation. But Ritchie, like most policemen, had little time for psychiatrists. Breaking the law was a deliberate act which had to be punished. Normally his moral debate went no further.

But normally he wasn't faced with the possibility of ending the career of somebody he'd once duffed up in Ratty Nellie's art classes.

In the distance a Salvation Army band played carols to ill-tempered shoppers battling through the streets on the day before Christmas Eve. Those of the murder squad who were not out on inquiries were in the pub or the canteen. Ritchie sat alone in the darkening office. He wished he had a cigarette.

12

THE second attempt to arrest Johnson was successful. He was naked in bed, alone after Alison had gone to work. Shocked into wakefulness by the crack of the breaking door, he had lunged for the nearest available weapon, a kitchen knife lying on the floor next to the debris of a hacked about loaf.

Hopkins smiled as he kicked Johnson's hand away from the knife. 'This time we *are* pulling you in. Get up.'

They wrapped him in a blanket and took him to the police station, leaving behind a search team. Johnson was hustled through a back entrance. He began to struggle, the blanket slipped away, and he was propelled naked into a cell. The blanket was hurled in after him.

'Give me my clothes, you bastards,' he yelled.

'They're needed for forensic examination,' said Fullalove. 'Oh, and Merry Christmas.'

Hopkins and Fullalove reported the success of the raid to Pryke.

'You didn't manage to fuck it up, then?' he said. 'Oh, I am pleased.'

'What about leaking it to the Press?' asked Hopkins.

Pryke nodded, then changed his mind. 'We'll leave it until after Christmas. That gives us forty-eight hours with Mr Johnson before anybody can interfere.'

Alison returned home bone-weary from the Christmas Eve rush and dreading the bleak prospect of a cheerless Christmas. She was homesick for the family she had broken with six months earlier.

There would be no celebrations with Johnson, who affected to despise such ritual jollity. He would not have bought her a present, although he might have stolen something. She had bought him General Guderian's war memoirs to add to his library of Second World War books.

Lodgers opened the doors of their rooms immediately her key turned in the lock. Alison looked from one to the other. 'What's happened?'

'The police took your man,' said an Irish woman. 'They came this morning, soon after you left. He had no clothes on. They took him down in a blanket.'

Alison found their room in chaos, but it wasn't their chaos. The floor was crunchy with tealeaf-flecked sugar where the police had been careless in emptying containers. Johnson's library of tatty paperbacks had been pulled down from their stack and jumbled on the floor. The mattress had been stripped and his clothes, which usually hung on a door hook, were gone.

She bit her knuckles in bewilderment. Johnson had told her after the abortive raid that he was in the clear.

From a phone box down the street she called Ridley police station. The operator told her to hold on. He called CID. No reply. He called the murder room.

'They're all out,' said Dave Nicholas, who had declined to join the party in the pub and was re-reading old statements, looking for inconsistencies.

'We've got Toe-Rag's bird on the phone, wanting to know if he's here. What do I tell her?'

'Pryke's orders are to tell nobody. Better stall her.'

Alison ran out of twopenny pieces and put in tenpence. She kept the earpiece pressed to her ear, not knowing whether she had been cut off, and not having any more change to ring back. The long minutes passed until there was the signal for more money. She hunted frantically in her purse, but the connection broke.

She walked and ran the mile to the police station. The desk sergeant told her to sit while he found somebody to talk to her.

Nicholas refused. 'Ring Pryke at the pub and tell him she's here.'

'I've done that. He said: "I thought you'd got your orders," and put the phone down, the bastard.'

'Well, I'm not doing his lying for him.'

Ritchie, returning from inconclusive interviews with colleagues of Sendle, hesitated when he saw Alison in the hall, plainly near tears. She looked up. 'Oh, Mr Ritchie. Please tell me if Ralph's here. I can't get any answer out of anybody.'

'Have you asked the station officer?'

'He says he doesn't know.'

'Hang about,' said Ritchie, and went behind the glass partition to the station officer's cubicle.

'What can I do?' said the sergeant after he had told Ritchie the score. 'Pryke'll have my guts if I say anything.'

Ritchie nodded. Out of the sergeant's sight he wrote a number on a piece of paper and folded it into a wad. ' 'fraid I can't help you,' he told Alison loudly. Dropping into a low murmur he said:'Go to a phone box and ring that number.'

Living with Johnson had taught her a thing or two, he thought, as she palmed the paper without a change of expression. He went to his desk at CID (General) and waited until the call came through on the CID ex-directory outside line.

'All I can tell you is that he's here. He hasn't been charged with anything and his clothes have gone to the forensic lab for examination. And don't let anybody know I told you. It's supposed to be secret.'

'How long will they keep him? And what's it about? Drugs?'

'No idea,' said Ritchie, who had revealed as much as he intended to.

Alison wailed. 'Christ. What can I do?'

'Get a solicitor, if you've got the money. Rostock's good but he costs.'

'I haven't any money.'

'I don't know then, unless you try Tommy Tompkins, you

know, the reporter who did the story about the raid balls-up. Press inquiries might make them move a bit, or at least issue a statement.' He extracted another promise from Alison that she would not reveal that she had talked to him, and cleared the line.

Tompkins picked up Alison in his car and they cruised round Ridley. By this time she had become suspicious of Ritchie's motives. Hesitantly she asked Tompkins' opinion of him.

'Straighter than most detectives,' he shrugged. 'He's not a Boy Scout, but he would't be in CID if he was. Not particularly subtle, and he'd need a reason to do the dirty on you.'

'It's not what Ralph says about him.'

The reporter laughed. 'Ralph's got no reason to love him, but then he picked the wrong bloke to be clever with. Ritchie can be ruthless if necessary.'

'So why's he helping me? Is he trying to use me?'

'Doubt it. Pryke's in charge of this case and if he was doing something devious it wouldn't be through Ritchie. No, Jack believes in justice beneath it all. Half his trouble's his wife, dreadful woman, she pickles onions by breathing on them. She's trying to get him promoted and all he wants to do is to go his own sweet way. If he thinks Ralph is being set up it'd be like him to do something about it, if only to spite her. What's your problem, anyway?'

Narked by the police denial of his raid story, Tompkins took pleasure in the prospect of tweaking Pryke's nose again. He called the murder room and got the long-suffering Dave Nicholas, who said wearily: 'If I knew what was happening I wouldn't tell you, but I don't so I can't. Pryke's your man.'

'He's in the boozer celebrating the birth of Our Lord, I suppose?'

'As you would expect of somebody so pious.'

Tompkins phoned Pryke at the pub. 'Well?' he said, after putting his question and waiting through a long silence.

132

'Well what?'

'Are you holding Johnson in connection with the murder?'

'No comment,' said Pryke and banged down the phone. 'If I knew who it was talking to Tompkins, I'd have his guts,' he told his cronies.

At midnight, the Nativity having washed in on a tide of alcohol, Pryke reeled over to the station. 'Bugger off,' he told everybody. 'I want to go through some papers.'

When he was alone he went to the deserted canteen and felt his way over to the refrigerator. In its cavernous interior, behind a heap of liver, he found the jar of PC James's blood handed over by the pathologist. Wrapping it with a handkerchief he took it back to his office.

Pryke got Johnson's jacket from the exhibits cupboard in the murder room and dripped a minute amount of blood on the right cuff. He wiped the blood bottle carefully and returned it to the refrigerator, and waited till the jacket dried on the radiator.

He worked on the bloodstain with spirit cleanser until he judged it to be in the state it would have been left in by a clumsy attempt at cleaning, and replaced it in the exhibits cupboard.

13

JOHNSON lay grey-faced and shivering in the cell. He had got used to the old socks and urine smell of the mattress, and the lingering odour of vomit on the blankets. He could smell sweat, but that was his own. Agonizing stomach cramps alternated with fits of shivering. His nose itched. He had a bruise on his right cheek which had been the result of the raging attack he had launched on the copper who had brought him a meal. Now they came in pairs, but the withdrawal pains had drawn the teeth of his aggression.

Earlier he had tried to counteract his misery by an exercise of will-power. He did press-ups and exercises until overcome by the cramps. Living from one minute to the next took all the strength he had.

The door opened. A policeman brought his lunch – chicken, sprouts, roast potatoes with leather skins. Another policeman stood behind the one bearing the food. Johnson eyed them with hatred. 'What's this shit?'

'Christmas dinner. We look after you here.'

'Stuff it,' said Johnson and turned to the wall.

'Hey,' he shouted as the door closed. 'When do I get out of here? What am I in for?' There was no answer.

The cells were as hushed as a terminal cancer ward. Johnson had been their only occupant since the last Christmas Eve drunk had been turfed out that morning. The cells had no windows and the lights were always on. Only the arrival of food gave Johnson a sense of time. Disorientation. That was the name of the game. He had experienced it before.

He banged on the door and a policeman asked what he wanted from outside. 'I want to see my girlfriend.'

'She's not here, and she's not been here.'

'You liar,' sobbed Johnson feebly. 'She must have been here.'

The copper laughed. 'Probably found some other feller for a bit of drumstick,' he said and was rewarded by hearing Johnson's fists pounding the door. Johnson was as unpopular with Uniform as he was with CID.

As the hours passed Johnson moved into a state of trance in which his craving for heroin and the sudden cramps were all that remained of reality.

Contrary to popular belief, there is no limit to the length of time a suspect can be detained without charge. The prospect of harsh words from a judge, or the availability of a lawyer to try to obtain a writ of habeas-corpus, are the only practicable limits to the power of the police to detain people.

Pryke let Johnson sweat until Boxing Day. He rang Hopkins in the morning. 'He's been without a fix for thirty-six hours and hasn't spoken to anybody. Go along with Fullalove and see if he's ready to cough. If not, soften him up a bit. He should be nearly ripe by now.'

Johnson, however, was in better shape than they expected. Knowing that they would expect him to do anything for a fix stiffened his resistance.

He watched warily as Hopkins led the way into the cell, followed by the aimlessly smiling, dark-haired Fullalove. The door closed behind them and Hopkins and Fullalove pulled down the folding bed opposite. They waited in silence for Johnson to speak.

'What's all this about?' he asked, eventually.

'You tell us,' said Hopkins.

'I don't know, so how can I?'

'We can wait. You're not leaving until you tell us.'

Johnson sneered. 'We're playing it like that, are we?'

'Like what?'

'Leaving me to break up out of a sense of guilt.'

'What do you feel guilty about?'

'I don't feel guilty.'

'What do you mean, then?'

'About what?'

'About feeling guilty.'

'I don't feel guilty. Stop trying to twist my words.'

Hopkins gave a short laugh: 'Hark at that, Ray. He's accusing me of twisting his words. Look, son, you said you were feeling guilty and I asked what about. Isn't that right, Ray?'

'Word for word,' said Fullalove.

'So what do you feel guilty about?'

'I don't feel guilty about anything.'

'Then why did you say you did? You must be feeling guilty about something.'

Johnson shut up. He knew that if he continued along these lines he would end up in a state of complete confusion.

'Well, come on. Tell us what you feel guilty about. You'll feel a lot better.'

Silence.

'Tell us why you feel guilty. You said you felt guilty. Why do you feel guilty?'

Silence.

'But you did say you felt guilty, didn't you? Or did we get it wrong? Didn't you say you felt guilty?'

Silence. The repetition of the word 'guilty' had a hypnotic effect. Johnson wanted to burst into speech just to break up the rhythm, but he knew it would merely expose some other weak point for Hopkins to work on.

Hopkins continued his monologue round the word 'guilty' for another ten minutes, but with a Herculean effort Johnson remained silent. Hopkins caught Fullalove's eye and gave a slight nod. Fullalove took over.

He leaned over to where Johnson was sitting, still draped in his blanket. His big right hand flickered out with the speed of a snake's tongue and slapped Johnson hard across the bruise on his cheek. 'You got that in a punch-up with a policeman, didn't you? You're not so handy when you aren't holding a knife and the policeman can fight back, are you? Fancy a fight with me, you toe-rag? I'd enjoy that. You're the hard man aren't you? That's your reputation isn't it? I think you're soft. Soft as shit.' He feinted another blow, this time to the opposite side of Johnson's face. When Johnson ducked Fullalove slapped the bruise again.

Johnson half-rose and Fullalove snatched the blanket away. 'Soft, I said. As soft as that horrible little white thing between your legs. See that, Hoppy? He's hardly a man at all, is he? No wonder his girlfriend hasn't bothered to ask about him. Gone to find herself a man with a real prick, I shouldn't wonder. I wonder what he does with it. Plays with himself all day, most likely. Hoping it'll grow big and strong and he'll be able to find out what it's for.'

Fullalove snapped his fingers: 'Do you think that's why he's a junkie, Hoppy? You know, sliding the needle in and out like he'd slide his prick in and out if it was big enough and strong enough and straight enough. I bet that's it. It's his substitute for being a real man.'

He made as though to pick up Johnson's penis between thumb and forefinger. Johnson's hands darted over his crotch. Fullalove changed direction and tweaked Johnson's nose, bringing tears into his eyes.

'See that, Hoppy? He's crying. Didn't I say he was soft? We've barely started and he's crying already. What will he do when the going really gets rough? Pretend to faint like a little girl, I expect.'

'God, you pig,' Johnson half-sobbed.

Fullalove cuffed him. 'Be polite when you talk to us, Toe-Rag. Say Sir.'

Johnson said nothing. He watched mesmerized as Fullalove

picked his shots. This time it was his right nipple. He tried to tear away but Fullalove held on. 'Say Sir,' he said.

'Fuck off,' said Johnson, and tore himself away, rolling on to the bunk clutching his chest.

Hopkins intervened. 'Don't be too hard on him, Ray. He's making up his mind. I think he'll help us.'

To Johnson he said: 'Look, Ralph. We've got to get this James case cleared up. Sooner it's done, the sooner we can all go home. Just tell us about where you hide your heroin.'

Johnson looked up. He was about to ask: 'What heroin?' when he remembered his resolution to stay silent.

A policeman came to the door. 'Phone call,' he said.

'I'll get it, said Fullalove, and left the cell.

Outside he lit up a cigarette, and leaned against the wall, listening. The 'phone call' had been prearranged so that one of them could be alone with Johnson.

Hopkins drew out a packet of cigarettes and offered one to Johnson, who refused it, although he craved tobacco. Hopkins took one out and put it between Johnson's lips and lit it.

'He's a bad bastard, is Ray,' said Hopkins. 'That PC who got killed was his cousin, and he's really upset. Never was very nice at the best of times, but now ... He'll get himself into trouble one of these days. I'd like to help you, but I can't if you don't give me some help. I don't want to see him sinking his knee into your balls. You don't have to say much. Just pretend to cooperate. Answer the questions without really answering them, you know what I mean? It's the sight of you sitting there mum while his cousin's in his coffin that's driving him crazy. He thinks you're sneering at him.'

Johnson said nothing.

'I can't help you if you say nothing. You've got to at least look as though you're cooperating. Listen, he's coming back.'

'The call was for you, Hoppy,' said Fullalove. 'Well, is he going to help, or have I got to get nasty?'

Hopkins shook his head. 'I've done my best, Ray,' he said

sorrowfully, 'but I can't get a word out of him.' He left. Fullalove started again.

'Hard as nails, aren't you? You know what you are? You're a challenge, that's what you are. And there's nothing I like better than a challenge. Stand up.'

Johnson ignored him. Fullalove's hand flickered out and took his upper lip between thumb and forefinger and hauled his head up. Johnson had perforce to follow. Fullalove's elbow swept into his ribs and Johnson collapsed retching on to the bunk. Another 'comealong' grip, this time Fullalove's broad fingers twisted into Johnson's hair, followed once more by the sweep of elbow into the ribs.

Fullalove stood over him. 'Stand up,' he said again, but Johnson scarcely heard him as he fought for breath. Fullalove's hand grasped him by the scruff of the neck, his fingers digging for the nerves. 'When will you learn that the time for games is over?' he whispered into his ear. 'We're going to get the truth out of you if it kills you. Now talk, you little bastard. Talk, if you want to get out of here with teeth in your head.'

Hopkins finished his cigarette and came back in. 'I told you he was nasty,' he said. 'He's a disgrace to the police force, I've always said that. Well, we're going to give you time to think it over. We'll be back soon.'

'Don't think we're finished,' said Fullalove. 'We've only just begun.'

'Think we're on a winner?' he asked Hopkins as they strolled across the road to the pub.

'Dunno. Pryke acts as though he's sure, but how much that's because he is sure and how much it's because he wants to be sure is anybody's guess.'

Fullalove digested this. 'Might be better not to stick our necks out too far,' he suggested.

'I'm not sticking mine out at all,' said Hopkins. 'A pint, please.'

'I wondered why you left me all the fun. Now my neck's out.'

'Yeah? Well mine's already out a mile over the shebeen. I'm not allowing Whaley two cuts at it.'

Alison braced herself as she walked up the short drive to the double bow-fronted house with the green roof. She heard quick, light footsteps answering her knock and a small, immaculate woman opened the door.

'Hello Mother,' Alison said.

Mrs Parker touched her daughter's face with a warm dry hand. Alison flinched. She loathed being touched by her mother. Her younger brother poked his head out of the drawing room. 'It's Alison,' he shouted back, and joined his mother on the doorstep. Her father, tall and ruddy with wire-wool hair and a stark white bristly moustache, wrapped his arms round her. 'Come in. We were just toasting absent friends, weren't we Richard?'

Alison looked round. Everything seemed strange although nothing much had changed. But the polished parquet floors and warm rich rugs seemed like unimaginable luxuries after the dirty splintered floorboards and filthy druggets of the succession of rooms she had lived in with Johnson.

Her mother burst into tears and sobbed on Alison's breast. It was the demonstration of love that she had dreaded. 'Don't,' she said, disengaging herself. 'Please, Mother. Don't.'

She huddled on the sofa, giving monosyllabic answers to questions, knowing her family were taking in her pallor and the stained clothes she wore and her unwashed hair, and hating them for it. She wished she was anywhere else, even suffering one of those paralyzingly boring days in the Arcade Cafe. 'Dad,' she said finally, 'I want to talk to you, alone.'

He led her to his studio and sat her in a window seat next to a bookcase piled high with architectural magazines. The walls were lined with photographs and artists' impressions of the buildings he had designed.

Parker got her a whisky and waited.

'I need some money. A hundred pounds.'

Parker's face hardened. 'Not for that junkie, I hope?'

'For a solicitor. The police have arrested Ralph for something he didn't do. They think he killed that policeman, but he didn't.'

'How do you know?'

'He ... he was with me that night.'

Her father winced. He knew that Johnson had not been her first lover, but the thought of that scum caressing his daughter's body, feeling between her legs, made rage rise into his throat. 'I don't care whether he did it or not. If they threw him into a cell and dropped the key down the drain, I wouldn't care. If you were in trouble I would give you a hundred pounds, or a thousand. But not a penny for him.'

He immediately regretted allowing his anger to rule him, but Alison did not protest. 'I know what you think of him. I don't even blame you. But he's on the verge of kicking heroin, I know he is. And when he does, he might surprise you, and a lot of other people, because he's intelligent and strong, forceful, and he could really become something. But it won't happen if the police keep on at him. He can't bear being pressured.'

Parker was unmoved. 'He's a crook. If he comes off drugs he'll just be a different kind of crook. I won't help him.'

Alison pleaded again, but her father's determination could not be shaken. Finally, she prepared to play her ace. 'Dad, give me the hundred pounds and I promise you I'll give him up, leave Ridley and go back to art school.' Having made the statement she was conscious of an overwhelming feeling of relief and she realized that she had been wanting to make that decision for weeks. She was sick of the half-life she was living, but Johnson's dependence on her had made the decision to desert him impossibly hard. Now she could save him and herself at the same time.

Parker followed up the offer quickly. 'You mean that? You'll leave him?'

'Give me the money, let me get him out of the hands of the police. I'll tell him I'm going back to Bristol at the beginning of term. He won't follow me. His pride wouldn't allow it.'

Parked nodded slowly. 'Against my better judgement, then. Will a cheque do?'

'Make it payable to Peter Rostock. He's a solicitor.'

'I know him. Nothing but the best for Johnson, eh?' he said sourly, but did as she said. 'Will you stay for dinner? Mother would be pleased.'

'God no. I couldn't stand that.' She saw the pain in his face and kissed him. 'Tell her what I've promised. That'll make up for it.'

14

ROSTOCK lived nearby. He looked at the cheque, listened to her story and promised to do his best. He had Pryke's ex-directory home number and called him.

'I'll see if he's in,' Mrs Pryke said. Pryke shook his head when he heard who it was. 'No, he's just this minute gone out, but I'll tell him you called.'

Rostock rang the police station and told the duty inspector that Johnson was his client and he wanted immediate access to him. Pryke also phoned, and learned of the call. Cursing he rang the pub.

'Has he coughed?' he asked Hopkins.

'Not a word. He's shtoom.'

'Then why aren't you keeping at him?'

'We gave him a good going over and left him to sweat a bit.'

'Right. I'm coming over. Rostock's on our necks and we've got to get moving.'

'Well,' said Fullalove to Hopkins, 'if Pryke can make him talk, he's a better man than I am.'

They finished their drinks and crossed over to the police station as Rostock's Jaguar was pulling up. Hopkins hailed him genially. 'Come to scrounge a Christmas drink?'

'Love to. But let me see my client first.'

'Who is the lucky man?'

'Johnson.'

'Really? Santa must have been good to him. An expensive brief like you in his stocking. He's Mr Pryke's client. Hang about, I'll try and get him for you.'

Pryke had slipped into the compound through the back entrance. 'Let's have this monkey,' he told Fullalove. 'I'll make him talk.'

Johnson was lying on the bunk, shivering under the sour-smelling blanket. He looked up at Pryke, who stared down at him for a full minute. 'I am Detective Chief Superintendent Cyril Pryke. I want a statement from you concerning the murder of PC Rodney James.'

Johnson turned his face to the wall. 'You can fuck off,' he said.

Pryke ripped the blankets off and hauled Johnson up by his hair. He banged his head against the wall. 'You murdering bastard,' he screamed at the top of his voice. 'I'll teach you to talk to policemen like that.'

He dragged Johnson off the bunk and up so that, naked again, he was staring into Pryke's eyeballs. 'Now tell me what you were doing in Kimberley Road when PC James saw you. And don't say you weren't there because we know better. You were seen. We've got witnesses. So don't give us any shit about being in bed fucking your tart.'

'Sod off,' Johnson said between his teeth. 'I don't know what you're talking about.'

He let out a strangled cry as Pryke's knee sank into his groin. Outside in the passage Hopkins and Fullalove were listening. The station officer was at the top of the stairs with a worried look on his face. Officially he was in charge of the station and could have ordered Pryke to desist, but he was reluctant to interfere with so senior an officer. He made up his mind. 'The name of the game is cover your arse,' he said and made a phone call.

In the cell Pryke had slammed Johnson against a wall. 'I'll tell you what you were doing there,' he said. 'You were there because it's where you hide your stuff, in the alley beside number 32. We've got the heroin you left behind in an envelope. It's got your fingerprints on it. The copper saw you coming out, recognized you and started to search you so you let him have it with the knife. That's right, isn't it? We're going to nail you and it's all the same to me if you appear in court with teeth or without. So cough, you bastard.'

'I'm not coughing anything,' Johnson said between sobs. 'You're trying to stitch me up 'cause you can't get anybody else. I've made the only statement I'm making. I was home in bed. Anybody who says I wasn't is a liar.'

Pryke moved in again and the white-tiled cell walls echoed to thuds and yelps and panted demands for Johnson to cough. The door to the cell block opened and Chief Superintendent Wallace, head of Ridley Division, entered casually dressed, and stood listening for a moment. In a few strides he was at Johnson's cell and saw through the inspection window the naked prisoner, on his knees, his head forced up by Pryke pulling on his hair.

Wallace threw open the door. 'I want to talk to you,' he told Pryke grimly.

'I'm busy,' Pryke snapped.

Wallace marched in and separated the men with two violent heaves. 'Get out,' he told the detective. For a moment Pryke looked about to hurl himself on Wallace. 'I wouldn't if I were you,' Wallace said between his teeth.

'You're interfering with my prisoner,' Pryke yelled, out of control. 'Get out of this fucking cell.'

'He isn't your prisoner, he's mine. This is my station and whatever happens here is my responsibility.' He took Pryke by the arm, almost as though the detective was the prisoner. 'You and me are going to have a chat.'

A chat was too private a description for the shouting match which followed. It could be heard through the closed door of a charge room until Wallace ended it: 'Either you get off the station or I'll enter a report. And deal with Rostock on your way.'

Pryke left the charge room snarling. Wallace followed, stopping to peep into the cell where Johnson was lying on the bed weeping from pain and exhaustion. 'Check he's all right. Call a doctor if necessary. And get him some clothes,' he told the station officer. 'And thanks for the call. You did right.'

Rostock was in the entrance hall chafing when Pryke came out. He noted the expression on the detective's face.

'Hello, Cyril,' he said, holding out his hand. Pryke, with studied offensiveness, ignored it and Rostock let it drop. 'I'd like a word with Ralph Johnson.'

'Why?'

'I'm representing him.'

'Have you any proof?'

'I wouldn't be here on Boxing Day otherwise.'

'That's not what I asked.'

'Why don't you ask him?'

'I have. He says he doesn't know anything about you and hasn't asked for a lawyer.'

'Ask him if he wants to be represented, then. Has he been charged with anything?'

'I'm not touting for business for you, and I don't answer questions from bystanders,' said Pryke, turning on his heel.

On his way out he said to Hopkins and Fullalove: 'Take Johnson to bits. I'll handle Wallace if he gives trouble.'

The way you handled him just now? thought Fullalove. To Hopkins he said: 'Play it by the book, then?'

'Is there another way?' asked Hopkins.

Pryke was displeased. 'Do you mean two experienced detectives, one of whom is supposed to be an interrogation expert, couldn't made a junkie talk? I suppose you topped him up with heroin at hourly intervals?' he said icily next morning.

Hopkins said stolidly: 'We questioned him intensively. He refused to go beyond his previous statements that he was in bed with his girlfriend at the time of the murder.'

'Why didn't you haul the girl in?'

'We had no orders to do that.'

'You'll need orders to wipe your arse next,' exploded Pryke. 'Go and get her.'

Hopkins dispatched two detectives to bring Alison in. On his return he found Pryke had received Rostock's notification that he intended to apply for a writ of habeas corpus.

'We need a holding charge,' said Pryke. 'Did you find any drugs in his room?'

'No Sir.'

'Are you sure? What about stolen goods?'

'No Sir.'

Pryke gave Hopkins a hard look. 'What's the matter, Hoppy? You're not cooperating.'

'I'm sorry, Sir. I didn't realize that. If you give me a specific instruction I'll do my best to carry it out.'

So that's the way it is, thought Pryke. The rats are manning the lifeboats.

Pryke's day did not improve. The two detectives who had been sent to find Alison Parker returned to say that Rostock had her under his wing. 'He says he will bring her in if we want but will insist on being present during any interrogation. What do we do?'

'Leave her,' growled Pryke, who still thought he had a card up his sleeve. The jacket had been sent to the forensic lab with a note asking for urgent typing of the blood. The answer would give him sufficient reason to hang on to Johnson and resist the writ of habeas corpus.

As it happened the Home Office lab, knowing the jacket was possible evidence in a police murder, ran a full series of tests instead of merely typing the blood and leaving everything else to take its turn. As a result they confirmed, of course, that the blood type matched PC James's but also pointed out that it could not be his because it was too fresh, recently dried blood giving off a different aura under the spectroscope than old blood.

That left the identity parade, and here Pryke used all the tricks he had learned in a quarter of a century as a detective. He brought in the 'witnesses' from Kimberley Road one by one during the day and left them in an anteroom whose only window looked out over the yard in which the parade was being held. The sole reading matter was the album of photographs of heroin users with, of course, identities and convictions on the back of each picture. After giving the witnesses time to mull over the album and get bored, the parade was set up with the maximum of noise and shouting to attract their attention while the men were got into line. Finally Johnson was brought out separately between two PCs and allowed to choose his position.

These precautions resulted in several of the witnesses identifying Johnson as a man they had seen acting suspiciously in or near Kimberley Road, but they still could not date their sightings near enough to the murder to give him the result he wanted.

'It's all a bit thin,' said the solicitor the police had briefed to resist Rostock's application. 'I wouldn't like to ask a barrister to go before a judge with no more than that.'

Frustrated, Pryke phoned Rostock. 'You can take Johnson away,' he growled. 'We've finished with him for the time being. But that doesn't mean he's in the clear.'

'No,' said Rostock. 'It means you've got nothing on him.'

At lunch it was noted that Hopkins and Fullalove were absent from Pryke's drinking circle. Now it was made up of a younger, amoral element. Pryke's Rats, they were swiftly labelled. They had sensed the situation and were gambling that Pryke would ride this crisis as he had ridden others. If he did, their promotion prospects would be enhanced. If not, perhaps they would be too junior to be noticed when the shit hit the fan.

Pryke allowed himself to be drawn on the progress of the case. There was no doubt Johnson was their man. He had been preening himself among the junkies, boasting he was making a comeback and warning that anybody who opposed him would end up 'as dead as a pig'. His alibi was thin. The smallest crack would destroy it. Pressure had to be put on Johnson and his bird.

What sort of pressure?

'Never give them any peace. Split them up. He's cock-a-hoop now, thinking he's got away with murder. That's fine. It'll hit him all the harder when he finds he hasn't. Alison Parker's the key. She says she was in bed with him. If only we can get her to say she is a heavy sleeper and would not have noticed if he left the flat during the night, then that opens up a chink in his armour.'

When Johnson left with Alison and Rostock, Tompkins and a photographer were outside the police station. He gave an interview in which he said he planned to sue for assault and wrongful arrest.

The celebration continued in bed. 'I thought you'd want to shoot up,' said Alison later.

'I'm off it,' he said grandly. 'Those bastards tried to break me by offering me a fix and I told them to stuff it. Now I'm staying off.'

He added: 'Take some time off work. I feel good now, but it'll be bad later and I don't want to be on my own.'

It *was* bad later. He tramped endlessly round the bed-sitter, his nerves screaming. He felt as though diamonds had been inserted in his bone sockets. Only the fact that Alison was there stopped him from going to his cache of heroin — for he also had his secret supply — and fixing himself. Her steady green eyes gave him strength. Having made his boast he did not want her to see him fail.

At night he dreamed of Fullalove saying: 'Do you think that's why he's a junkie, Hoppy? You know, sliding the needle in, like he would slide his prick in if it was big enough and strong enough and straight enough?'

'I'm glad that pig's dead,' he said one morning when he was half awake.

'What?' said Alison.

He opened his eyes. 'I dreamt I was back in the cell.' He got up and started walking again.

After two days he felt the crisis was over.

'Come on,' he told Alison.

They went out. Johnson looked back out of force of habit, and realized he was being followed. At the main road they jumped on a bus as it was moving off and the detective ran back for his car. Johnson stopped the bus with a tattoo on the bell and they jumped off, ignoring the conductor's shouts. He led Alison to a graveyard and felt behind a gravestone which marked the last resting-place of a Victorian family. He found the packet which had been stuck down with adhesive plaster and opened it out. Four tablets, each a sixth of a grain of heroin, nestled in his palm.

Johnson looked at them curiously, as though it was the first time he had seen such things. 'Time to give the fishes their fix,' he said, and took them to the river which ran alongside the cemetery. It gave him an odd pang voluntarily to throw away something around which his life had revolved for so long. They disappeared immediately in the thick, brown water, and Alison giggled to think of the fish stoned out of their minds.

Next day Alison returned to work. An hour later she was home again with her cards and a week's money. 'Sacked for absenteeism,' she said. 'I told them I had a bad period but it didn't make any difference. I don't understand it. There are plenty of girls with records worse than mine.'

Gotobed rang the detective at the store where Alison had worked. 'That's one I owe you,' he said.

'I'll get a job,' Johnson said. At the Department of Employment office he was offered a job as a labourer at the cement works.

'Who do we know there?' asked Pryke.

'The head of Personnel was in the Job before he took his pension,' said Clegg.

'Good. Give him the word.'

In the beginning was the word and at the end was the word. The word was put out and made flesh. Johnson signed on the dole again.

'We'll get out of Ridley,' said Johnson. 'I'll get a job in London and call you when I've got a room.' Alison nodded, remembering her promise to her father. Term would start soon, but no need to tell Johnson yet.

Johnson got a job as a hospital porter, but not a room. He travelled back on an old ticket, dodging the inspector up and down the corridor. Wearily he emerged at Ridley, ready to give up his old ticket at the barrier, confident that in the scrum of passengers the collector would not have time to look at the date. Before he got to the barrier men loomed up on either side of him. Strong hands clamped over his wrists to prevent him throwing anything away.

'Come along, Toe-Rag,' said Clegg. 'We want a word with you.'

Two hours later he was released on £25 bail. There was derisive laughter in the canteen from Uniform Branch. 'You say he's killed one of our men and the best you can do is nick him for fiddling a fifty-bob ticket?'

'Nothing to do with me,' said Ritchie. But he was CID, and one of the enemy.

Pryke's Rats were huddled in a corner. Their conversation stopped when anybody went near and started again when the outsider was out of earshot.

'That's the level we're down to,' said Nicholas, gesturing at them. 'Dreaming up sick little schemes to break Johnson.'

Ritchie had stopped for a cuppa before going to Sendle's home. He had been there every day since his conversation with Hagley but Sendle had not returned. Pryke refused to put out a call for him. 'Johnson's our man,' he growled.

On his way out Ritchie went to his own desk in the CID

(General) office. A message said: 'Mick called. Will phone again at twelve.' That must be O'Hanlon. Ritchie had not heard from him for several days.

'Thought you must be dead,' he told O'Hanlon, when the call came in. 'Didn't I tell you to report daily?'

He cut Mick's protests short. 'A week I haven't heard from you, so that's a week's ban for the girls. If I hear they've been working in that time I'll nick the lot of you.'

'Have a heart,' protested O'Hanlon. 'Haven't I got news for you, about the murder and all?'

'Well?'

'One of my sisters, Kathleen, knows a boy who hangs round the Arcade Cafe. He's called Turnip because he's got a big head and a very white face. Turnip told her how this junkie feller with a foreign name reckoned he would get Ralph Johnson life and that sort of shit. Said he had led the law to where Johnson kept his H near where the policeman was murdered. Kathleen's here. Do you want to talk to her?'

Kathleen, the youngest of the O'Hanlon girls, had a soft voice that made Ritchie think of convents and confessionals. She went through her conversation with Turnip. No, Turnip had not said whether the heroin cache was planted by Stolz.

'All right,' said Ritchie at last. 'Tell Mick he's drawn a two-day sentence.'

'Can't you make it a month? My feet could do with a rest.'

'Only your feet? Look after yourself, Kathleen.'

Ritchie made out a report of his conversation and entered it. Now it was out of his hands. But if he happened to run into Turnip it would be reasonable to ask some further questions.

He did happen to run into Turnip, after waiting an hour outside the Arcade Cafe. He grabbed the lad by the shoulder. 'Hello Turnip. And how is life treating you?'

Turnip twitched and turned. 'Hello Sir,' he said in his polite West Country accent. 'Things are just fine.'

Ritchie noticed his pinpoint pupils. 'Been shooting up?'

'No Sir. I've left all that behind me Sir.'

'Tell that to the probation officer. What has Stolz told you about the murder?'

'Which murder would that be, Sir? The policeman? I can't recall Wally saying anything about that but if I do you can rely on me to call you Sir.'

'If you don't I'll take you to the station. At the station we will take a urine sample. If in that urine sample we find traces of heroin I shall charge you with unlawful possession. Have you heard of that technique, Turnip? Isn't science wonderful?'

'It is indeed, Sir. It does occur to me now that I may have heard Wally speak in particular of the subject, but I have difficulty in recalling exactly what he said.'

'Take your time. I'll walk home with you. The longer we are together the more likely we are to be seen, so that when you do tell me the more likely it is that people will put it down to you.'

'Yes Sir. This is in confidence, is it, Sir? I won't have to give evidence?'

'You have my word,' said Ritchie, who had every intention of breaking it if necessary.

'It was on Christmas Eve. Alison had come to the cafe looking for Toe-Rag Johnson. After she went Wally said he'd been arrested. Well, there was a cheer because nobody likes Toe-Rag very much, Sir, and Wally said we could thank him if he went down for life because he told the police where to find Toe-Rag's H.'

'Did he say definitely it was Toe-Rag's or did he say or imply that he had planted it?'

'He said just what I told you, Sir. The only other thing he said was it paid Toe-Rag back for the time four years ago when he tipped off the pigs ... Ouch ... I'm sorry Sir ... the police that Wally was carrying.'

'Where's Wally now? He wasn't in the cafe.'

'I think he's keeping out of sight. I believe he is nervous now that Johnson has been released.'

'Goodbye Turnip,' said Ritchie. 'And keep your mouth shut if you don't want us checking your wee-wee. Tell me if you hear any more.'

'I will Sir. Thank you Sir.' He waited until Ritchie was out of sight and cut off to Wally's home. He knocked on the door. There was no sound. 'It's me, Turnip. I'm alone.'

Stolz opened the door and peered warily down the passage before admitting Turnip. 'Got any stuff? he asked urgently.

'A grain. Five quid.'

He watched Stolz shoot up. 'If you knew what that cost my nerves. Ritchie pulled me when I was carrying. I was shitting bricks that he might search me, but he didn't. He was asking me about a rumour that you'd stitched Toe-Rag.'

Stolz turned a frightened face to him. 'What did you say?'

'Told him I knew nothing about it. He told me to ring if I heard anything.'

'Bloody hell. I was only joking. I wouldn't stitch anybody, not even Toe-Rag. You know that, don't you? We have to stick together or the straights get us.'

'Sure,' said Turnip, and extracted a promise that Stolz would not reveal that he had been tipped off. 'You know what Ritchie's like when he's got it in for somebody.'

'No sweat. I won't let you down.'

As soon as Turnip left, Stolz phoned Pryke. 'I thought you were going to look after me?' he said with hysteria rising in his voice. 'Ritchie's been asking Turnip about me. I tell you I'm not going to court if I'm not going to be looked after. Toe-Rag will kill me if he finds out.'

Stolz was shaken by the venomous blast he got from the other end. 'You'll do what you're fucking told if you don't want to spend the next few years in a cell,' yelled Pryke. He slammed the phone down. 'Time to settle with Ritchie,' he said to himself.

15

SENDLE was back. The groundfloor curtains were drawn but light filtered through them. Twitching curtains on both sides of Sendle's house caught his eye. Frank and the neighbour on the other side were forsaking the television for what they hoped would be a real-life drama on their doorsteps. Ritchie wanted to disappoint them.

Sendle answered his ring and surveyed him bitterly for a moment before admitting him to the front room, much of which was taken up by a grand piano. His holiday did not seem to have done Sendle much good. His straw-coloured hair was dry and lifeless and his face was an unhealthy white.

'I heard you had been asking questions about me. Couldn't you have waited until I got back?' he asked.

'I didn't know where you were. When you are on a murder inquiry you can't wait around, you know. If you had told me about you and Rodney James we could have got it over and done with weeks ago.'

'But I told you all I knew.'

'Alwyn, you didn't. There's a lot more for you to tell me, about the concerts you went to, and particularly those you went to with him alone, and what you did with the time you spent together, and when you last saw him.'

At last Sendle told Ritchie to sit down. 'All right, I did know Rodney quite well. He went to concerts with the music club. Eventually he dropped out. He never said why, but I presumed he just lost interest. After that he was just another boy in the school. And that is all there was to it.'

Ritchie's eyes hardened. 'You're lying and I can prove you're lying. See here, I've spoken to Rodney's father about you. He told me that he had to break up a relationship between you and Rodney. I've spoken to Hagley. He told me that Rodney went alone with you to a concert and after that he dropped out of the concert trips. So don't tell me that there was nothing to it.'

Sendle conceded a point. 'Yes, we did go alone to one concert. But that was because everybody else dropped out through illness. A mere accident. Surely the fact Rodney never went again proves there was nothing in our relationship?'

'It shows you were trying to camouflage your relationship and that, in turn, shows there was something wrong with it. It was after the concert that Rodney's father discovered you were seeing each other and put a stop to it.'

'He was making a fuss about nothing and both Rodney and I told him so. He accepted that, didn't he? Do you think he would have let matters rest there if what you are suggesting was true?'

'What am I suggesting?'

'I don't know. Some sort of filthy homosexual relationship, I suppose.'

'You don't approve of homosexuality?'

'Of course not.'

'You've changed since we were at school, then?'

Sendle swallowed and said nothing.

Ritchie named the two gay pubs. 'Do you ever go to them?'

'I've been to one.'

'I know you have. You know it's a homosexual meeting place?'

'No, I didn't. I have nothing to do with that sort of thing.'

'Not even in a public lavatory in Bradford, three years ago?'

Sendle swayed and Ritchie thought he was about to faint. Yet could the question have been so completely unexpected? Sendle recovered and stared silently at the floor.

'You see, Alwyn? There's no point in pretending. Now tell me the truth about your relationship with Rodney.'

He shook his head. 'There wasn't one,' he said stubbornly.

'It's not good enough. Since he left school he's been lying to his parents about where he spent his free time. He told them he was going out with Desmond Hagley, but Hagley hasn't seen him in months.'

'I don't know where he went. It wasn't with me.'

Ritchie sighed and drew out the picture of James in school uniform. 'A barman identified him as being with you in the pub on a number of occasions in recent months. Now will you be sensible, or am I going to make more inquiries which will include talking to your headmaster and telling him you've got form?'

Sendle stiffened. 'You can do whatever you've got to do. I've got nothing to add.'

Ritchie shrugged. 'I'm sorry Alwyn. You give me no alternative unless you come clean about you and Rodney and satisfy me that it couldn't have been you who killed him.'

Sendle half-smiled. 'I was alone in this house at the time of the murder. Will that be sufficient proof for you? No, I didn't think so. You make your inquiries. I've nothing to add. All you'll succeed in doing is blackening Rodney's name.'

'Goodbye, Alwyn. I'll see you soon.'

'That wouldn't surprise me. Goodbye, Jack.'

Next morning Ritchie barely had time to lay the report of his conversation with Sendle on Nicholas's desk before Pryke, who had left his office door open so that he could watch for his arrival, ordered him in.

'Pack up,' he ordered brusquely. 'Hand everything you've got on your plate to Gotobed. You're going back to general duties.'

Ritchie stared at Pryke in disbelief. 'Why?' he demanded.

Pryke said levelly: 'Why? Because you're insubordinate, that's why. I made it clear that you were to confine your efforts to PC James's background. You disobeyed my orders. I've no use for disobedient policemen and particularly not for men who can't play their part in a team effort. You've been pulling on a different rope to the rest of us almost since the case started and I've had a bellyful. And I'll give you one more order. You are to stay out of this case. If you hear anything you will pass it on in the proper manner but if I hear of you making inquiries you will be out of CID. Is that understood?'

'Y-yes Sir,' stammered Ritchie.

'Right. Get out.' Pryke returned to the papers on his desk and Ritchie wandered, dazed, into the main room.

Dave Nicholas looked up from Ritchie's report. In cold handwriting it had not looked much to account for the air of suppressed excitement with which Ritchie laid it on his desk, but Nicholas knew that such reports often did not tell the full story. An experienced detective could sometimes tell that there was something more than met the eye in a witness or an item of information, even if he was at a loss to explain why.

'Well, what's behind it?' he demanded. Ritchie's shell-shocked expression registered on him. 'What's up?'

'I'm off the squad,' said Ritchie. 'Posted back to general duties.' He started to tell Nicholas the story. There was a tap on his shoulder. It was Pryke.

'Don't stand gossiping,' he said genially. 'There's plenty to be done in CID (General). There's a very worrying spate of milk bottle thefts in Totley.'

Ritchie packed up in silence. He told Gotobed of his suspicions about Sendle. Gotobed didn't seem very interested. 'You're making a lot out of an incident which happened years ago. You don't even know if Sendle and James had it away together.'

'No,' said Ritchie. 'I've just got a feeling.' He knew that Gotobed would not risk Pryke's wrath by continuing the investigation.

He reported to the inspector who was dealing with the ordinary crimes of the day with a skeleton staff. 'Fallen foul of Pryke, have you?' Ritchie nodded. 'Easy enough to do, I suppose. Well, you won't be idle here. You can take back your case load for a start. I doubt if it's been touched.' He gave Ritchie another thick file.

'You can add this to it. Some old boy gave power of attorney to a friend when he went into hospital. He died and the friend siphoned £4000 off the estate in three months. See if you can get a fraud charge out of it.'

Alison's father answered the door to her ring. 'I've come to dinner, Dad,' she said. 'And to talk about art school.'

Parker looked at her coldly, almost with hatred. 'Why are you really here? To recover that filth you left?'

Alison recoiled from the violence in his tone. 'What filth? What do you mean?'

'Don't play the innocent. You know what I mean. The cannabis you hid in the pot plant when you came to beg a hundred pounds from me. It isn't here. The police have got it.'

'But I didn't leave any cannabis here. I didn't have any on me. What do you mean, the police have got it?'

'They raided us,' shouted her father. 'Police cars all up the road, with their lights flashing and neighbours packed six deep round our gate. They took me and your mother and Richard to the police station. Your mother in her dressing-gown. They dragged her out of bed where she had gone with migraine. They didn't charge us, thank God, although they said they could have. When they heard you had been there recently they said you must have left it when you came round.

'Well, I think so too, you little bitch. Your mother nearly had a nervous breakdown. She's been in bed ever since. I suppose you know how they search women for drugs? It must have happened to you often enough. Well, what do you think your mother felt having a doctor's hands prying around inside her?'

'Honestly Dad, I didn't leave it. It was a plant. They're using you to try to break Ralph and me. Make him confess to a murder he had nothing to do with. They got me kicked out of my job, then when he got one they had him kicked out of that. Now this.'

Into Parker's mind came a vision of Clegg saying: 'You know the worst thing about junkies? They become really fertile liars. To hear them you'd think they never touched the stuff, that all the drugs in this country are bought by policemen to plant on innocent youngsters.'

He made an inarticulate sound of contempt. 'Planted! That's what the police told me you would say. Well, I saw Sergeant Clegg take it out myself. They weren't even here about drugs. They were looking for the knife your boyfriend used to kill the policeman.'

'He didn't. Honestly.'

'Honestly? Do you know the meaning of the word? Go away Alison. Stay out of this house.'

Alison sobbed. She had been expecting a joyless evening, but she was hungry and penniless. It was Johnson who had persuaded her to come. That way she at least would get a square meal. Her visit on Boxing Day had reawakened a desire for normal existence, for carpets underfoot, meals eaten off decent china and cooked in an oven, not boiled or fried off twin hotplates. She was overcome by a sense of her own futility against the might of the police which could even prevent her from making peace with her family.

Parker softened a little. 'It's Johnson's fault. I don't care what he has done or what he hasn't done, but he's destroying you. Leave him and I'll help you all I can.'

Alison nodded and turned away. Parker watched her go. He felt as though he had hurled her back into the depths of the pit she was trying to climb out of. He went to his study and wept.

Ritchie had worn off his venom in a blast of hard work on the suspected fraud case. He had interviewed the family and their accountants and the suspect. The latter he had chatted to genially, contriving to give the impression that he found the whole case a little too much for him. He had taken a statement which he was sure contained enough demonstrable lies to prove a minefield if the suspect came to rely upon it, and was on his way into the station to type up the details.

Cruising into town from Totley he saw a skinny-legged blonde aimlessly walking in the same direction. There was something about the set of her bowed head which range a bell. He slowed and watched his rearview mirror for a glimpse of her face and stopped, 'Alison,' he called.

Alison looked up hard-eyed. She recognized him. 'Mr Ritchie?'

'Why are you crying?'

She turned away, unable to answer. Ritchie came close and she muttered: 'As if you didn't know.'

'I don't. Tell me.'

'That raid on my Dad's house. Are you telling me you didn't know about it? It must have been a right giggle for you and your mates, especially that bit about carting my mum off to a Black Maria in her nightie. And planting the cannabis in the pot plant. Really subtle that was. You're sick. All of you coppers, you're sick.'

'It was nothing to do with me. I'm not even on the case any more. You'd better fill me in.'

Alison filled him in, not just about the raid but about her losing her job and Johnson losing his and being chucked out of their digs and being unable to find any others. 'Your lot, they're just bloody sadists.'

'Thanks.'

'Oh, not you, perhaps,' Alison said grudgingly. 'You were the only bloke who was decent when Ralph was arrested. But if you had been in on the raid, would you have stopped them from planting the shit?'

'They wouldn't have done it in front of me. That's why I'm off the sqad. I don't like the way they're going about this. If Toe-Rag did it I want him nailed right.'

'He didn't do it,' said Alison fiercely. 'I wouldn't stay with a murderer. You've questioned him over and over again and you've still got nothing on him.'

'Toe-Rag's capable of murder all right,' said Ritchie

dispassionately. 'He's got all the qualifications. And you know those books about the Nazis and concentration camps he collects? It's surprising how often psychopaths have libraries like that. It's a form of pornography. But it doesn't mean he did this one. The brass may have good reason for thinking he did, but if so they're keeping it to themselves.'

Ritchie stopped. He had been talking more to himself than to her, clarifying his own feelings about the case. But he had said more than he intended.

'Where will you sleep tonight?'

'I don't know. I was going to scrounge a meal and a bed with my family, but Dad chucked me out because of the raid.'

'Have you broken with Ralph, then?'

Alison shrugged. Her mind felt dead. 'I don't know. I'm not sure how much more I can stand of this type of living. Will you drop me near the cinema? I told Ralph I'd meet him there if I didn't stay at home. Dad wanted me to leave Ralph and now he's thrown me back to him. Stupid, isn't it?'

As they approached the town centre Ritchie said: 'Don't take this wrong. I'm not trying to interfere. But if you do need somewhere to stay for a day or so, while you try to sort yourself out, I'll fix it with a friend. But only you, not Ralph. If he turns up I'll throw you both out.'

'Why?' asked Alison bluntly.

Ritchie hardly knew the answer. A gesture of defiance to Pryke, perhaps. And that niggling accusation of cowardice by Eileen. Perhaps he was just a fool.

Lamely he said: 'I don't like the thought of you tramping the streets. Another thing, Toe-Rag likes to turn his girls on. If you haven't already started now's the time — when you're at your lowest ebb — you might be tempted.'

'You're wrong.' There was triumph in Alison's voice. 'Ralph has turned off.'

'I'll believe that when I see it,' said Ritchie, drawing up at the roadside. He pulled out a loose-leaf notebook and scribbled

Eileen's name, address and phone number. 'Anyway, take this and use it if you want to. Don't forget, just you.'

Alison read the address and put it in the pocket of her coat. 'Thanks, Mr Ritchie. I'll get out here.' She slipped quickly out of the car and disappeared up a side-street.

Johnson paced outside the cinema, ill with cold. He had not recovered his jacket from the police and under his dark-blue overcoat he had only a chilly nylon shirt. He was in the grip of a deep hunger for a fix. It was not the physical agony of a few days earlier but an intense yearning for the sensation of warmth and wellbeing which would mask his cold and hunger and desolation seconds after the needle penetrated his scarred veins and the plunger descended.

He had waited an hour outside the cinema before Alison arrived. He had not found a bed. 'The law's put the word round that they'll raid any place we stay,' he told her.

'What now?' Alison asked hopelessly.

'Find an empty house and doss. God it'll be cold.'

Alison felt faint. She had eaten nothing all day. 'Dossing?' she said. 'Oh no. I can't stand it.'

Johnson peered closely at her. 'You've been crying. Another row with your family?'

Alison told him about the raid. To her surprise he laughed. 'Middle-class bastards. That'll show them the other side of Dixon of Dock Green.'

'No it won't. They believe what the police told them, that it was me who left the shit in the pot plant.'

'Yeah? Well sod 'em. Let's find somewhere to shack up.'

The page of Ritchie's notebook with Eileen's address on it drew her hand. As she touched it a vision of a hot bath, food and clean sheets flashed into her mind. She turned irresolutely.

'Come on,' Johnson snapped.

Alison made her decision. 'I'm not coming.'

'What? Where do you think you're going to sleep tonight?'

'I've been offered a bed.'

'That's great. We can share it can't we? Where is it?'

'No we can't. I was offered it strictly on condition I took it alone. I'm sorry, Ralph. I can't face sleeping rough. Not in the middle of winter.' Alison leaned against a wall. The disgorging cinemagoers, on their way to pubs with New Year's Eve extensions, looked curiously at her and Johnson. He took her by the arm, glaring his hatred at the crowd. Alison broke free.

'I can't. I'm not going. Look at me, Ralph. I'm just a middle-class bitch like my mother. I want a bed to sleep in and a place to wash, and warmth. I can't take being thrown out of one bed-sitter after another, living like a rat, being thrown out of jobs.'

Johnson grabbed her arm again. 'Come on,' he said between his teeth. 'Come on or I'll hit you.'

A young man leaving the cinema with his girlfriend heard the threat. 'You can't do that,' he said.

Johnson stared at him challengingly. 'Can't do what, fuckwit?'

'You pig. Leave her alone,' said the young man's girlfriend.

'Better a pig than the mouse you're with,' said Johnson reckless with rage. The man flushed and came forward. Johnson moved inside the swinging fist. He punched the man in the pit of the stomach and brought his heel hard down on his victim's instep. He went down screaming and the girl swung a leather handbag at Johnson's head. He snatched it and tossed it under the wheel of a bus.

There was a gasp from the gathering crowd at the deliberation of the act. Hostile faces closed in. Johnson realized Alison had gone. He broke through the circle and fled round the corner.

Alison heard the pounding feet and started running even before she glimpsed Johnson over her shoulder. She ran a hundred yards, but knew she could not shake him off and turned to face him, breast heaving and arm thrown up to ward off any blow. It did not come and she lowered her guard. Johnson's face was contorted with misery and anger. 'You're letting them win,' he shouted. 'They beat me up and took away my H and I spat in their eye. Now you're giving in.'

'I don't care any more, don't you understand. Leave me alone.'

Johnson tried to talk gently to her, to persuade her to go with him. He took her by the arm but she tried to drag away from him. Losing patience he twisted her arm behind her back until her tendons were at full stretch. 'Walk,' he said.

She walked. Johnson guided her to a row of old houses converted into offices which housed a variety of small businesses, and into a service lane. 'Wait here,' he said. 'If you run away I'll tear your arm out.' She nodded spiritlessly.

He searched the row for an unlocked window and found one that somebody had forgotten to latch. He went back for Alison and they climbed into a basement.

The way to the ground floor was unbarred and they found themselves in a three-room suite of offices. They listened to the silence of the building for fifteen minutes before Johnson would risk moving around. There was one inner office with no windows. They closed the door and put on the light. 'It's fine,' he said. 'Carpet on the floor, electric fire and kettle. We can be comfortable here. Dossing isn't so bad if you know your way around.' Alison found a chair and said nothing. Later they cleaned up in the lavatory, shivering in the cold. Johnson watched Alison closely, but she showed no inclination to make a run for it.

He found tea and milk and mugs and they sipped the brew in silence before lying down to sleep on the carpet, Johnson tight against the door, head pillowed on his overcoat.

He woke in daylight with a momentary fear that they had slept too long. But the building was still silent. There wasn't even any traffic noise, and he realized it was New Year's Day. Alison was still breathing heavily. Johnson looked at her. He caressed her head and bent down to nuzzle her ear, but in the angle of her head and neck his breath, malodorous with hunger, bounced back at him. He grimaced and went out of the room to rifle the building for money or valuables.

All the doors were locked as he climbed to the top floor. There were prints on the wall, and wallpaper which demonstrated careful choice. It looked like a staircase to a private flat. He listened at the door for several minutes then rapped sharply. There was no sound. The door was hinged to open inwards and it flung back with a crash when Johnson hurled his weight at it.

The flat seemed to be a man's pied-à-terre. The refrigerator held a bottle of wine, some eggs and bacon, and there were some tins of expensive foods, pâté, lobster, game soups and the like in a cupboard, drinks in a cocktail cabinet. The single bedroom held a large double bed and a rack of girlie magazines. It was a pity he had not known about this the night before, thought Johnson. The wardrobe held men's clothes, bigger than Johnson's size, but he stripped and took underwear, a shirt and sweater. On a shelf he found an expensive Japanese camera, and leaning in a corner a fishing rod. These could be hidden on his person when he and Alison left, so he put them aside.

He was about to shut the door when he wondered at a pile of rags on the floor of the wardrobe. He felt under them and brought out a locked, polished mahogany box. He found a screwdriver and broke it open. Under a cloth lay a .22 target pistol with moulded grip and a hundred rounds of long-nosed ammunition.

Johnson caressed the gun. He looked at the name. Walther. German. He spent ten minutes struggling to insert an empty magazine before finding out how to do it, hefting the gun, marvelling at its balance. He cocked it and pulled the trigger a few times and wished he could fire it. What sort of noise would it make, he wondered, and regretted that he dared not risk firing it in the building.

With a start he realized that he must have been up in the room for nearly an hour. Gathering up the camera, the fishing rod and the gun, he ran downstairs. 'Alison,' he called. 'See what I've found.'

There was no answer. The room they had slept in was empty and the window by which they had entered was open. 'Alison! Alison!' screamed Johnson, dropping the gun and the camera. He found a note in the room where they had slept. 'Ralph,' it said. 'I'm leaving you. If you try to come after me I'll call the police. I'm sorry. Alison.'

It was Turnip who was first with the news. He rang Ritchie, who was working on the holiday. 'Toe-Rag's on the loose with a gun,' he said. 'He says he's going to kill Alison.'

Ritchie extracted the story from Turnip. Johnson had turned up at Stolz's flat, where Turnip had spent the night. 'He seemed half-dazed, wanted to know if Alison was there. Christ, you can see everything there is to see in Stolz's flat with one look, but he kept asking. Stolz was shitting in case he had come about the H you found, but he didn't mention it. Stolz offered him some and Toe-Rag sat there looking at it for about two minutes before he took it and shot up. I've never known him hesitate for a second before. Then he pulls out this shooter and says he's going to kill Alison and then himself. A copper as well, if he can, he said.'

Ritchie called Eileen and found that Alison was there. 'Tell her not to budge until I give the word,' he ordered and phoned Pryke.

Pryke's satisfaction at the turn of events could be heard over the phone. 'I'll be round,' he purred. 'Do you know where the girl is?'

Pryke noted Ritchie's fractional hesitation before the denial. Could he be knocking Alison off? he wondered. 'Order a lookout for her too. And instruct everybody to approach Johnson with caution. I'm coming in. Order out everybody who's qualified on weapons.'

Gotobed, the force's rifle champion, came in with an alacrity that suggested he had been dreaming of this moment since the case began. He was followed by Hopkins, Fullalove and others. They awaited the arrival of Wallace, who, as head of station, held the armoury key. He listened to Pryke coolly. Their relationship had not mended since the Boxing Day row. 'It's not another cock-up, I suppose?' he asked insultingly.

'There's no cock-up,' gritted Pryke. 'There never would have been a cock-up but for you and interfering bastards like you.'

Wallace shrugged. 'I'll leave it to the Chief,' he threw over his shoulder as he stalked to his office.

Whaley, called from home, was also reluctant to issue guns. Ritchie was called in to recount his conversation with Turnip. Pryke fumed while a squad car was sent for Turnip and Stolz. Only when they told the same story did Whaley consent to the issue of weapons. Ritchie was not included.

'Get back to whatever you were doing,' Pryke growled.

Ritchie watched the men as they loaded their guns and checked the action. There was satisfaction in their faces. Gotobed stared down the sights of his favourite .22 target rifle. 'Let's hope he shoots it out,' he said meditatively. There was a low growl of agreement.

Ritchie could stand it no longer. He left the station and drove to Sendle's house.

16

It was the milk bottles on the doorstep — four of them — that alarmed him. And the drawn blinds. There was no answer to his knock. Peering through the letterbox he could see newspapers and mail scattered in the hall. He went next door. Frank appeared in his leisure wear of baggy flannels and singlet.

'Happy New Year. Still at it?'

'Yeah. Do you know where Sendle is?'

'No idea. Ain't he in?'

'Doesn't look like it.'

'Gorn visiting, maybe, like at Christmas.'

'Then he's forgotten to cancel his milk and papers.'

'That's unlike him. Very careful bloke, as a rule. Come to think of it I ain't seen him since that night you called.'

Ritchie got a tyre lever from his car, sliding it up his sleeve out of Frank's openly curious gaze. He went round the back and jimmied open the locked gate with a sharp crack. The curtains at the rear were also drawn. Doors locked. He broke a window pane, undid the catch and let himself in. 'Alwyn?'

No answer.

He searched the house. It was tidy but there were paper ashes in the grate of the sitting room. In the kitchen, plates and cutlery were laid out ready for use. They were covered by a film of dust. A book lay open face down on the fridge.

A muffled explosion made Ritchie jump. It was the boiler, activated by a thermostat. Milk and papers not cancelled, plates and cutlery out, boiler on? Ritchie's skin crawled.

He found Sendle in the bath, naked, facing the door with eyes open. His body from the navel down was stained brown except for his drawn-up kneecaps, which were white. The plug was in but the water had seeped away except for a small puddle, trapped by his body, which had evaporated leaving a darker stain. The gases of decomposition had swollen Sendle's stomach. A fat and unseasonal bluebottle did a victory roll before landing on the stained razorblade which Sendle had used to cut his wrists.

Ritchie gagged and got out of the bathroom.

On the landing he paused for thought, wondering how the hunt for Johnson was progressing. He took out his personal radio and switched to the channel the force used for more confidential communications. From the instructions being issued he judged that the main effort was moving away from the built-up areas. There was nothing to indicate any firm sightings. He decided to search the house, keeping the radio on.

Sendle's bedroom kept whatever secrets it held. So did the study next to it. Half his attention on the radio, he flicked through the papers in the desk. Bills, school memoranda, clippings from educational magazines, nothing of a personal nature except letters from his parents. Ritchie noted the address so that they could be informed of their son's death.

(' ... report of shooting southern perimeter of Monk's Wood. Persons not involved. Alpha, Lima and Yankee, can you take it?')

Ritchie hesitated for a moment before resuming his search with greater urgency.

The sitting room was tidy, but the drawer of a Welsh dresser showed signs that it had been cleared out. There were no private papers. Ritchie leafed through a photograph album. The later pages were torn as though pictures had been ripped out.

On his knees in front of the fire grate, Ritchie examined the ashes he had seen earlier. The shadow chemical images of photographs showed through on some of them. Others were probably letters. Sendle had neglected to crush the ashes, probably unaware that forensic laboratories had developed the reading of burned papers to a fine art.

Ritchie saw an unburned corner of pale-green writing paper. Gingerly he extracted it. It contained a few meaningless letters. He could delay no longer. He crossed the hall to the phone, kicking over a wastepaper basket in his haste. Glancing down at the debris he saw a pale-green envelope.

Ritchie scrabbled through the contents of the basket until he found a twist of the green writing paper, screwed up so tightly it bespoke passion and anger. Aware that every second wasted was putting lives in peril, he nevertheless smoothed it out.

It was from Rodney James, dated the day before his death:

Dear Alwyn,

I am sorry I have to write this letter. I did hope you wouldn't make things difficult for me. We simply can't go on, surely you see that? Discovery would end my career. I don't think I can ever forgive you for threatening to reveal our relationship. And please, don't call me at the police station again.

Ritchie called the police station and asked for Pryke. 'Not here,' said the operator. 'Word's just come in that Toe-Rag's holed up at Harvey's Farm wanting to shoot it out. One of our men is wounded. Pryke's on his way there now.'

If Johnson had known who it was had sicked the police on to him, Stolz would not have survived the morning. He was looking for somebody to kill before falling to a hail of bullets. Or that was how he saw it.

He knew Wally or Turnip would call the police and decided to move out into the country, away from his usual haunts. He was unable to think clearly. The heroin had hit him hard after his several days' abstinence and his brain was a confusion of emotions in which resentment, hatred and excitement were uppermost.

Twice he made cover ahead of a cruising patrol car. When he

reached the cover of woods he sat on a tree root, hand on the butt of the pistol in the waistband of his trousers.

A man walking his dog stared curiously at Johnson, who looked back insolently and did not reply to the New Year greeting. The man turned away. Johnson watched him out of sight, mentally taking aim at the broad cloth-covered back. He got up and jogged through the woods until he reached a field where bullocks were grazing.

He looked round carefully and drew the pistol, sighting it on the head of the nearest bullock and then dropping his aim to fire under. He shot single-handed, squeezing the trigger luxuriously.

The kick threw his aim. The bullet smashed the bullock's jaw and it reared up, its moo turning into a shocked bellow. Johnson watched, petrified, as it broke into a stumbling run, its legs buckling. The other bullocks fled from the sound of the shot and the sight of the bloody apparition, its broken jaw wobbling as it ran.

Johnson vaulted a gate and ran after it. The field was large, but the wounded bullock ran in a loop and Johnson eventually caught up with it. He fired the whole magazine at close range, but the light .22 bullets were not capable of killing it quickly without hitting a vital spot. Johnson sobbed as he clumsily reloaded. The bullock was dying now, kneeling, its head on the grass, drowning in its own blood. With a shudder Johnson fired point-blank between its agonized eyes. The animal's blood-sheened flanks quivered and it rolled onto its side and died. Nearby a dog howled.

Johnson looked up and saw the man who had been walking his dog watching in horror from the edge of the field. He dragged the dog away and disappeared into the cover of the trees. Johnson fired a shot in his general direction and ran the opposite way.

He fled headlong into the country, not knowing or caring where he was heading, and kept going for ten minutes before he stopped to catch breath. He rested only for a few minutes before following a cart track round the breast of a hill. Turning a corner he came face to face with a Panda car whose driver had been unfortunate enough to be away from his radio when the warnings about Johnson being armed and dangerous were broadcast. He had been found by the man with the dog and was looking for the lunatic who had been shooting at cattle.

The car stopped and the door opened. Johnson drew and fired, two-handed now, and a dark heap slid out of the car on to the road. Johnson scrambled up the rise and ran on. He paused to look back and saw the wounded man on his knees reaching into the car for the mouthpiece of his radio. Johnson watched for a second, wiping his mouth with the back of his gun hand, then jogged on, seeking a refuge.

He found one, a tumbledown house on a bridlepath. He went round the back and opened the kitchen door. An old man was seated in front of a log fire. He looked up and started to speak. Johnson raised the gun from his side into the old man's line of vision and the words tailed off.

'Are you alone?'

'My wife's in front,' the man said in a strong Wiltshire accent.

'Call her. Don't worry. You won't get hurt if you're sensible.'

The man was silent. Johnson's voice hardened. 'Call her. Do as you're told or I'll shoot you.'

Still the old man hesitated. 'We've no money,' he said. 'We're pensioners.'

'Listen Grandpa. I'm hungry and I want food, and that's all I want from you. Do I have to kill you to get it?'

'Ma,' called the old man. 'Ma, come here.'

A fat old woman answered crossly: 'What'm you want?' The old man pointed at Johnson with his chin and the woman's hand went to her breast.

'Get me food. Bread and cheese will do, but hurry.'

She set out the food and milk and stood back.

'Right, you can leave now. Go down the road and wait. There'll be a police car along soon. Tell them I'm waiting for them here. My name's Johnson.'

They took coats from the kitchen door. 'You won't damage the house, will you?' said the woman, anxiously. Her husband pulled her away and Johnson watched them out of sight.

Munching food he looked round the house and decided to make his stand in the main bedroom. It occupied the full width of the house, had windows on three sides and commanded the bridlepath. He locked the downstairs doors, took his food up, locked the bedroom door and took post in a dormer window.

He did not have long to wait. A squad car inched along the bridlepath and stopped a hundred yards away, well out of pistol range. A policeman got out in full view, confident in the knowledge that their quarry was unable to touch him. Another policeman got out with a rifle. He cocked it and took up a position where he could use the car's roof as an aiming rest.

Johnson felt calm and unafraid. The heroin buzz had long passed and fatalism had taken its place. Through the leafless hedges he could see moving blue lights and a minute or two later a convoy moved up the path and parked at the side. A movement to his right caught his eye and he saw that a police Land Rover had found a route across the fields. It too stopped out of pistol shot. Leisurely, deliberately, the police set up their siege. A crash from downstairs told him that men approaching on the blind side were into the ground floor.

Out in front a tall silver-haired man seemed to be in charge. He took the microphone of a loudspeaker van.

A granite voice rang out: 'Ralph Johnson. Ralph Johnson, please signify if you can hear me.' Johnson did not move, reasoning that it was a trick to make him reveal his position. If he was within a quarter of a mile he could not have failed to hear.

'Ralph Johnson, this is Arthur Whaley, Chief Constable of South Wessex Constabulary. We have this house surrounded. Walk out unarmed and no harm will come to you. We do not want any shooting.'

'Speak for yourself,' muttered Gotobed, who was lying in a prone firing position, his .22 rifle snuggled into his shoulder and close to his cheek, trigger finger taking first pressure. It was loaded with hollow bullets which in field conditions had dropped an attacking lion cold but had also shot an enraged monkey in the head without the frangible round exiting. Gotobed also had a .300 with solid bullets available in case it proved necessary to kill Johnson through the wattle and daub walls of the cottage.

Dozens of eyes scrutinized the cottage behind binoculars or telescopic sights. In the house Johnson turned to see if any targets were creeping into range at either side. The movement caught several eyes. Fullalove tapped Gotobed's shoulder. 'Dormer window, right-hand side.'

Whaley tried again. 'Ralph, come out and surrender. You will not be hurt. We have policemen in the house and we are prepared to wait as long as necessary.'

Another car rumbled up the bridlepath and Ritchie got out. Pryke saw him first. 'Who told you to come here?'

Ritchie ignored him. 'Is Johnson in there?'

'Trapped upstairs,' said Hopkins briefly.

'What's the plan?'

'Get back to your duties,' said Pryke, mottling.

'Sit and wait, unless he does something silly. Blow his fucking head off if he does,' said Fullalove.

'Get back to the station,' said Pryke, raising his voice.

'We can't,' said Ritchie. 'He didn't kill James.'

'You still pushing that line?' said Hopkins. 'He tried to kill another of our men today.'

'Get back to the sodding station or I'll have your stripes,' roared Pryke. 'How many police killers do you think there are in this town, anyway?'

'One,' Ritchie yelled back. 'And he's dead in Ridley.'

Silence fell.

'It's James's old music teacher. They were having a homosexual affair and James wanted out. He wrote a note which makes it clear that Sendle was taking it badly. The day after that he was murdered. Do you think that's a coincidence?'

'Then what do you think Johnson's doing up there, threatening to shoot any copper who comes within range, if he's not the killer?' Pryke blasted back, but Ritchie had seen shock and fear in his eyes. 'I've told you to go back to the station and you've disobeyed. Well you're out of CID and if you've any sense you'll get out of the force. I'm sick of your fucking fairytales.'

The knowledge that Pryke was on the retreat, at least mentally, brought weeks of frustration boiling out of Ritchie. 'Fairytales, is it? You've been making up fairytales for weeks now. Why's Johnson up there? You've been out to break him. Maybe you've succeeded. If anybody gets killed today it'll be down to you, you fat drunken bastard.'

Pryke swung at Ritchie, who ducked the blow but lost his footing in the mud. He fell against Pryke and hauled him down. The two men rolled over and over, punching, gouging and kicking at each other.

Whaley was unable to believe his eyes. He came over at a run and hauled Pryke up by his coat collar. 'Get up, you damned fool. Get up. Stop this.' Ritchie got up, covered in mud and breathing heavily. Whaley looked from one to the other. 'What sort of force is this where two experienced officers at a major incident scrap like a couple of Irishmen in a pub? Go back to the station, both of you. I'll deal with you later.'

'Sir,' said Ritchie, 'this is important.' He drew out James's crumpled note and passed it over, explaining the background.

'God,' said Whaley explosively. 'This is all we need. We'll be crucified.' He looked at Pryke with a hatred which was not unmixed with triumph. 'You aren't fit to be a traffic warden, let alone head of CID. You're suspended from duty until the inquiry. If I were you I'd occupy myself writing out a letter of resignation.'

'Give me that letter,' ground out Pryke. He read it. 'It doesn't amount to a confession of homosexuality, let alone proof of murder.'

'Then why did this man commit suicide?' asked Whaley,

witheringly. 'Oh, get out of here. You can stay, Ritchie.'

Nobody looked as Pryke got into his car but, as though by common consent, everybody held his breath until his car lurched into the road.

'What now?' said Whaley, almost to himself. It was vital to bring Johnson out alive if possible. He had sent for CS gas shells, but they could not arrive before nightfall. Suppose Johnson came out shooting before then? Would there be any option but to kill him? Rubber bullets? They would also take some time to procure and were only effective at fairly close range, a considerable risk against a man with a gun.

'Sir?' He looked up. Ritchie, still coated with mud, asked if he could make a suggestion.

'Let me go in and speak to him.'

'I suppose you could work your way round the back. We're holding the ground floor. You could shout through the door, but don't let him get a shot at you through the woodwork.'

'No, Sir. Let me make an open approach. I'll tell him about Sendle. If he knows he's not a murder suspect maybe he'll come out.'

'But he faces a long term for that policeman he shot today.'

'We owe him his life, Sir. He probably wouldn't be up there but for us.'

Whaley compromised. 'Call him on the loudspeaker and ask him to wave if he will speak to you.'

Ritchie went to the loudspeaker van. 'Ralph,' he called. 'This is Jack Ritchie. I want to talk to you. I have important news. I am coming to the house unarmed. Wave if you agree.'

Binoculars trained on the house. There was no movement. Ritchie repeated his call. He saw a movement in the window. 'He waved, Sir,' he told Whaley. Gotobed, squinting through his telescopic sight, disagreed. 'He just shifted position and caused the curtain to flutter,' he said, but Ritchie was already marching forward.

He plodded down the muddy path, eyes on the dormer window, willing Johnson to stay his hand. There was a sudden movement and splintering of glass. Ritchie threw himself sideways. Something plucked at his coat and two sharp cracks sounded simultaneously, one from the window and one behind, from Gotobed's gun.

'Get back,' called Gotobed. 'I've got you covered.'

Ritchie scrambled to his feet and swerved out of range. 'Did you get him?'

'Don't think so,' said Gotobed. 'He just whanged one off at you and dodged back. If I'd been using the .300 I'd have had him.'

Whaley stepped over. 'That's enough, Sergeant. You did your best for him. We'll just have to play it whichever way it breaks now.'

But Ritchie was not ready to concede. 'I know where his girlfriend is,' he said, ignoring Hopkins' and Fullalove's quick hard glances. 'Maybe he'll listen to her.'

'Worth a try,' Whaley assented. Ritchie called the controller and told him to send a car for Alison at Elieen's address. Hopkins said quietly: 'You take some terrible chances. You'd better be sure what you're doing. Your neck's riding on this.'

Ritchie, who did not need telling, nevertheless swallowed hard and sat alone in his car waiting for Alison. The first car to arrive brought Tompkins, however. He looked into Ritchie's car but took the hint when Ritchie stared straight ahead. Whaley gave him a brief statement and Tompkins drove off to file his story. Hopkins gave instructions not to allow him beyond the road when he came back.

Alison took in the scene, white-faced and saucer-eyed. 'What's happening, Mr Ritchie? Are you after Ralph?'

Rapidly Ritchie explained the situation. She took the microphone: 'Ralph, this is Alison. Please listen to me. Let Mr Ritchie come and talk to you. He's got some important news. Please, Ralphie, hear what he's got to say.'

'There's no point in asking him to signal his willingness to talk, Sir,' Hopkins said to Whaley. 'We can't trust him. Ritchie had better say his piece over the loudspeaker.'

Ritchie saw Tompkins' car at the road. He gestured to it. 'He'll hear everything. It'll be in the papers tomorrow. I must speak to Johnson face-to-face.' Without waiting for permission he started back down the track, feeling huge and vulnerable. He got to the spot where he had been shot at. Nothing happened. Was Johnson waiting for him to come closer? He mastered an urge to sprint for the dead ground under the walls of the house.

He got to the wall without incident and exhaled his pent-up breath. The ground floor was packed with armed men led by Inspector Dale. On the upstairs landing two men with drawn pistols stood flat either side of the door. Ritchie rapped on it. 'Don't shoot. I'm coming in unarmed.' He tried the handle. The door was locked.

'Ritchie,' said Johnson in a low voice, 'tell whoever's on the landing to leave the house.'

Dale contacted Whaley by radio and the men were withdrawn.

'OK, Ralph. They've gone.'

A key turned in the lock.

'Come in slowly. Shut the door behind you and lock it. If anybody else tries to get in I start shooting.'

17

FEAR like ice in his stomach, Ritchie did as he was instructed. Johnson, pale and wild-eyed, was standing flat against the wall three yards away, the gun aimed at Ritchie's head. After the door was locked Johnson spoke again.

'Sit on the bed and say your piece. Remember, I'll kill you if you try anything.'

Johnson went back to the dormer window, ducking under the sill, and sat on the floor. There was pain in his face and he was holding the gun left-handed. The right sleeve of his sweater was ripped and soaked with blood. Gotobed had not, after all, missed completely. Ritchie knew Johnson was right-handed. He noted it as a small thing in his favour if necessary.

Johnson did not like Ritchie's cool sizing up of the situation. 'Spit it out,' he said impatiently. 'What's this good news? Are you going to offer me twenty-nine years inside, instead of thirty, if I give myself up?'

'Don't be silly, Ralph. Come out without any more shooting and there'll be no thirty years. The policeman you shot today isn't dead. He's wounded in the shoulder and in no danger.'

'Pity,' said Johnson. 'Two dead pigs for whatever happens to me. It wouldn't be such a bad exchange.'

Ritchie smiled at the bravado. 'Don't start with that. We know what happened the night the policeman was killed. There's no point in any more fairytales.'

'What's happened to Alison?'

'She came to us. I found her somewhere to stay.'

'She coughed, did she? I knew she would if you got her alone. Soft cow.'

Something in Johnson's tone frightened Ritchie more than his dead eyes and the gun in his hand. 'Yeah, she's told us all there is to know,' he said cautiously. 'Still, you can't complain. Did you proud for a month, didn't she?'

'I'd like to kill her as well.'

'As well as what, Ralph?'

Johnson ignored the question. 'Ralph, is it? Whatever happened to somebody called Toe-Rag? Is it just that he never had a gun in his hand? Is that why he was Toe-Rag and I'm Ralph?' His gun hand dropped and momentarily Ritchie thought of jumping him. The eyes flickered sharply and Ritchie realized Johnson had been testing him.

'Yeah,' Johnson said, raising the gun and looking Ritchie in the eye, 'I killed that copper.'

'No, Ralph,' said Ritchie amiably. 'You can forget that. We know what happened. He was homosexual and his lover killed him and committed suicide.'

Johnson stared at him in astonishment. A slow smile broke over his face and developed into a chortle and then into a full laugh of savage glee.

'I forgot,' said Johnson. 'You had faith in me.'

Ritchie sat on the bed looking foolish and bewildered. Johnson revelled in the sight. 'So he was queer, was he? If I'd known that I'd have offered me bum instead of knifing him. Sorry to disappoint you, Ritchie, but it wasn't lover boy who did him, it was me. You'll find the knife I used down a drain in Bygrave Street.

'It was bad luck, that's all. I'd scored in London and came back on the paper train without a ticket. I didn't want to get off the train at Ridley because there are hardly any passengers at that time of night and it's almost impossible to slide out without being spotted, so I pulled the communication cord about half a mile out and jumped off.'

That sentence stripped away Ritchie's illusions. He remembered the line in the old woman's statement, the one who had spotted Tilt's car, about being woken up by a train stopping. He felt paralyzed with horror.

'I had six grain on me and I didn't want to walk across the town centre with that, so I went to this alley I had used in Kimberley Road and hid the stuff behind a loose brick, came out and walked straight into this fucking copper.

'I was about to land him one and scarper when he shone this torch on me and said "Johnson". Well, if he knows me there's not a lot of point in me belting him, is there? So I told him I just went down to take a leak but he says: "What were you hiding down there?" and starts dragging me down the alley.

'Well, with six grain down there, and a knife on me, I know it's another long sentence ahead, and I didn't fancy that, did I, not having just come out. So I pulled out the knife and let him have it in the ribs. He let go and staggered a few steps out into the road and drops. I pissed off smartish like and dumped the knife when I was well away.'

Ritchie was shattered and his face showed it. Johnson smiled blandly. 'Made a bit of a prick of yourself, haven't you?'

Ritchie moved convulsively. Johnson raised the gun a millimetre and said: 'Yes, please.' Ritchie subsided.

'I don't believe you,' he said. 'You might have been able to lie your way out of it, but not Alison.'

'Dead right. You should become a detective. What I did was, I fixed it so she didn't really have to lie. It happened when, early hours of Thursday? When I got home she was asleep. I went to bed without waking her and in the morning I said I'd got home at about one o'clock. She'd gone to bed before that so she didn't know the difference.

'We heard about the murder from a friend of mine who said there was a big round-up of suspects going on. I told her that if I was pulled in they'd try to say I did it because of having been out and not being able to prove when I got home. So you know what I did? I just got her to change Wednesday night for Tuesday. Everything we said happened on Wednesday night did happen, but the day before. That way she didn't have to lie. We've got no telly so she couldn't be tripped up over the programmes and I warned her that you would come to me and say she'd coughed and go to her and say I'd coughed but if we stuck to the story we'd be OK. And we were, weren't we?'

'So it was your heroin we found?'

'Don't be soft. As if I'd leave six grain of H near a dead copper. That'd be a dead give-away, wouldn't it? Somebody must have planted it. You most likely. But who tipped you off about me using the alleys?'

'I don't know. It was Clegg's tip.'

Johnson thought. 'Stolz, then,' he said savagely. 'So that's how he wriggled out of that possession charge. It was Stolz, wasn't it?'

With the bitterness of humiliation Ritchie said: 'Does it matter? Is there one of you who wouldn't sell the other for the price of a fix?'

Johnson's mouth twisted and he stared venomously at Ritchie. 'Yeah?' he said. 'So what do *you* get for stitching somebody up, Ritchie? A pat on the head from Hopkins? A good mark on your record? And how many people have you done it to?'

'Prison's full of villains saying they've been framed.'

'And some of them are right, aren't they? Tell me, Ritchie, now that I've got this gun and you're being so polite, the first time I got nicked for possession over that jacket, who put the heroin dust in it?'

'You did.'

'No. I never carry heroin loose on me. You put it there, didn't you?'

'You're out of your mind.'

'Am I? Well, I'm going to kill you if you don't tell me.' He raised the pistol until Ritchie was staring down its barrel. He swallowed and licked his lips. 'All right, if you say so.'

Johnson held his aim. 'I ought to kill you,' he said. After a long moment he lowered the gun.

'What do you expect me to say with a gun on me?'

183

'It was the truth. You know it, and so do I. I don't have to prove it in court. I just wanted to hear you admit that you're a criminal, just like me.'

Johnson was silent for a moment, then his lips twisted into what passed for a smile. He put on a plummy voice. ' "You cannot be allowed to take the law into your own hands." That's what the judge said after I carved up that bastard from Bristol who tried to move in on me. So it's one law for me and another for you, is it Ritchie?'

Ritchie didn't answer. Hate for Johnson was boiling up inside him. Fury at himself for having gone out on a limb for him wasn't far behind.

He watched Johnson coldly, measuring the distance between them. He watched a sheen of sweat break out on Johnson's forehead. The left hand holding the gun drooped fractionally. Johnson's eyes had lost their sharpness.

Ritchie hurled himself across the room and kicked the gun out of Johnson's hand. It hit a side wall and fired, the bullet bringing a small shower of plaster down from the ceiling. Ritchie dived for the gun and picked it up.

From downstairs a voice called. 'Jack. Are you all right?'

'I'm OK,' he called back. 'We're coming out.'

To Johnson he gestured with the gun. 'Get up, Toe-Rag,' he said.

Half-dazed, his face colourless, Johnson started to obey, dragging himself to his feet. As his head moved into the frame of the window Ritchie had a sudden vision of Gotobed lying there, his rifle tight into his shoulder and his quarry moving into the crosswire of his sights. He would have heard the shot, and seeing Johnson would assume Ritchie had been the target.

Ritchie opened his mouth to order Johnson down again.

There was a high, hard crack and Johnson spun, blood gouting from his neck. The door crashed flat and Dale led his squad into the room. They leaped into marksmen's crouches, holding their guns two-fisted and weaving to find a target.

Dale lowered his pistol and stared expressionlessly down at Johnson. The blood flow slowed down as the heart gave its final pumps.

'It's all over,' he said into his radio. 'Johnson's dead. Ritchie's OK.'

It was another hour before the ambulance bumped down the track with Johnson's body. Ritchie manoeuvred Alison into his car. Tompkins was trying to talk to him. He brushed the reporter off. Tompkins, desperate for a good quote, persisted. 'Get out, Tommy,' Ritchie said with a patience which only just held hysteria in check. 'For once in your life leave well alone.' The reporter stood back and watched thoughtfully as Alison and Ritchie drove away.

'Now tell me,' commanded Ritchie with icy intensity. 'What happened the night the copper got killed? And I want the truth this time.'

Alison looked at him, looked away and looked back, suspecting a trap. 'What truth?'

'THE truth. The one and only truth, goddammit. I suppose you know the meaning of the word?' Ritchie yelled, his voice almost breaking into a scream. He grabbed her by the arm, barely seeing the road ahead. 'Was Johnson out that night? Did he come back while you were asleep? Did he tell you to transpose Tuesday for Wednesday? Tell the truth.' Only Alison's gasp of fear prevented him from driving the car into a ditch.

'Did he tell you that?' she asked in a quivering voice.

'Yes, that's what he told me. Now, is it true?'

She hung her head. 'Yes, it's true.'

'Oh my God.'

'He didn't do it, did he? The murder, I mean.'

'It looks like it.'

'I'm sorry, Mr Ritchie. I believed him when he said he didn't. He was afraid of being stitched up. He said you'd once ... '

'I know what he said.'

After a while Alison said: 'What will they do to me?'

'Charge you with obstructing the police, maybe. Odds are you'll get probation. You might be held for a couple of days. Do you want to get anything from Eileen's?'

'My washing things, then, and a change of clothes.'

While Alison was upstairs collecting her things, Ritchie told Eileen what had happened. 'So Pryke was right all along,' he concluded wearily.

She was baffled. 'But how did he know? Was it just luck, or did he have more information than you?'

'Luck? Perhaps. Johnson did use that alley to hide his stuff, but the drugs we found weren't his. Did Pryke know that? Probably he did. I expect he worked Stolz over until he had sorted out fact from fiction and went on from there.'

'Then it was still a frame-up. Pryke was just lucky he was framing the right man?'

'I suppose so. But a lot of crimes get cleared up on just the sort of information we had about Johnson. Convictions for violence, a connection with the area, a credible motive, an alibi resting on a girlfriend. Take four factors like that and any copper would go to town on a suspect. How far Pryke was manufacturing a case as distinct from putting on the pressure is something only he can answer. And he won't.'

'He still did wrong.'

'Did he? Well, he got it right in the end, and I got it wrong. So he's home and dry and I'll be facing a list of disciplinary offences that'd go twice round the block. Disobeying orders, concealing a witness, having a punch-up with a senior officer, plus a few things that I'll have forgotten but Pryke won't.'

Eileen was silent. Ritchie sat at the table trying to work out how he had got into this mess. It seemed ludicrous now that he had ever sought to prove Toe-Rag Johnson's innocence.

Eileen broke the silence. 'Was Johnson right? You know,

about you putting the heroin in his jacket that time?'

Ritchie sighed. 'Yes,' he said heavily. 'Johnson was right.'

'But why did you do it?'

'Why? Johnson was going around being a flash monkey. Telling everybody he'd got the pigs on his side. We weren't going to have that so we busted him. He always was a cautious bastard. Never kept his stuff around, so we helped it along.'

'Then you're as guilty as Pryke?'

'For Christ's sake. He was turning kids on to drugs. He was an evil bastard, so we put him out of the way.' Ritchie knew it sounded indefensible and so did Eileen. She did not press the point.

'What will happen to you?'

'Chucked out of CID and busted to PC for sure. Out on my arse if I'm unlucky. On the beat if the Chief's feeling kind.'

Ritchie suddenly thought, but how would they know he had got it wrong if he didn't tell them? Only he and Alison knew the truth and she would surely keep quiet. And Eileen. He could rely on her, couldn't he? And who would be any worse off, except Pryke, if Johnson had died in silence? Nobody.

Nobody, that was, except for Gotobed, who would believe he had killed an innocent man, and James's parents, who would believe their son had died as a result of a squalid homosexual affair. And Sendle's parents, who would be told their son was a murderer.

He looked up. Eileen was watching him. Alison's footsteps were sounding on the stairs.

Eileen saw them to the door. She kissed Ritchie. 'Come back, whatever happens,' she said.

He nodded and drove to the police station to take Alison's statement and write out his report.